The Broken Horseshoe

Coleman Black is stumped by a string of murders and robberies near the boom town of Deadwood. His best friend, hired to transport money from a cattle sale, is among the victims. Cole is desperate to find answers but, with no clues to go by, the killer could be anyone.

When Cole decides to take some inspired advice from a new friend, he has no idea that he is being led directly into the line of fire. Meanwhile, the killer smiles as he silently waits in the cover of timber, his rifle already aimed at Cole's heart. . . .

The Broken Horseshoe

Billy Hall

A Black Horse Western

ROBERT HALE · LONDON

ISBN 978-0-7090-8946-9

Robert Hale Limited
Clerkenwell House
Clerkenwell Green
London EC1R 0HT

www.halebooks.com

Typeset by
Derek Doyle & Associates, Shaw Heath
Printed and bound in Great Britain by
CPI Antony Rowe, Chippenham and Eastbourne

CHAPTER 1

Danny Hyatt didn't swagger. Not to the extent that you'd call swaggering, anyway. Still, there was sort of an inner swagger in the way he walked. It just naturally emanated from a supreme sense of self-confidence. Maybe it was more than just confidence. It was almost an air of invincibility. He knew he was up to any confrontation he might be called upon to face. He knew that whatever it was, he would emerge the victor. He always had, even when the odds had been overwhelming.

Lesser men might have become arrogant. Or careless. Danny was neither. He was just supremely confident.

Even now, faced with an adversary six inches taller and nearly sixty pounds heavier, he was confident. That didn't mean he didn't take the man seriously. The man's broad shoulders and lean hips betokened both strength and speed. The scars on his knuckles were more numerous and thicker than those on his face. He was a fighter, and he was used to winning.

That much was instantly obvious to Danny.

Maybe that was what caused Danny's self-confidence to irritate him so deeply. It was evident that the younger man was not in the least intimidated by him. Most men were. Even when they tried to hide it, most men avoided any confrontation with Harvey McElroy.

Donnelly's Saloon Number Six was busy. All the saloons along Deadwood's single street were busy. It was, after all, a mining town. It was a boom town. Gold drew men in staggering numbers, and they were all thirsty, it seemed, all the time. Their seemingly insatiable appetite for booze, women, and sudden wealth drove the engine of frantic prosperity. That frenzy had lined the large gulch with buildings, many clinging precariously to the edges of hills. It had transformed a small slice of wilderness into what had to be the longest, narrowest town ever built.

Danny had ridden slowly into town, studying the scrambled mass of buildings that lined the narrow gulch. It had only one street. That was all there was room for. Everything in town was strung out along that narrow canyon for three miles. If there had been any side streets, they would have been too steep to climb, let alone build on.

The message from his boss had been to meet him at Number Six. Nobody bothered with the 'Donnelly's' part of the name. Nobody bothered with the names of any of the other saloons that squatted along the busy street. They just acquired a number when they opened, and that's what they were known

6

as. Number Three had closed when its owner pulled a gun on the wrong man, so there was no 'Number Three' now. Other numbers would be left vacant before long, it was certain, but the new ones that came along would still bear the number that indicated the order in which they opened for business.

He tied his speckled gray gelding to the hitchrail and strode into the saloon. There was only one space open at the long bar, made of rough lumber. He stepped up to it and rested his elbows on the bar. At the raised eyebrows of the bartender, he said, 'I'll just have a beer.'

He dropped a coin on the bar as he said it. The bartender hesitated noticeably. 'Uh, that there's where McElroy was standin'. He just stepped out back to relieve hisself.'

Danny shrugged. 'Somebody else will have to do the same afore long, I 'spect. He'll find a spot soon enough.'

The bartender shrugged enough to indicate it was Danny's problem, not his. He set the beer in front of him and swept the coin off the bar.

Danny took a sip of the beer, then wiped the foam off his upper lip with the back of his other hand. Holding the beer in his left hand, he turned around. He hooked his elbows on the rough bar and looked around the room. His boss was nowhere in sight. Just as well. He could stand to have a casual beer and maybe a little conversation while he waited.

That was when Harvey McElroy returned. He

walked purposefully toward the spot he had left at the bar, then hauled up short at the sight of somebody else occupying that space. He cocked his head slightly to one side and blinked rapidly twice. 'That's my spot,' he declared.

Danny looked him up and down coolly. 'That so? It was plumb empty when I walked in.'

'I was just out back takin' a leak.'

'Beer does that to a fella,' Danny observed agreeably. 'There'll be several spots open up within five minutes for the same reason, I'm guessin'.'

McElroy scowled at the unexpected response. 'That there's my spot,' he asserted again.

Danny looked him up and down again, slowly, deliberately. 'That don't fit,' he said.

'Whatd'ya mean?'

'I mean you look like you're a fit workin' man. You don't look nowhere's near enough of a barfly to have a special spot with your name on it at the bar.'

'That's my beer, there,' McElroy declared, ignoring Danny's comment.

'Oh!' Danny responded. He reached for the mug of beer and handed it to the big Irishman. 'Here you go.'

McElroy's face turned deep red. 'I don't want the beer! I want my spot at the bar where I was.'

Danny grinned. 'Life's sure enough that way, ain't it? It's plumb hard for a man to get what he wants anywhere, these days.'

McElroy answered with a swift right, aimed for the insolent youngster's face. He was fast. He just wasn't as fast as he thought he was. As if knowing exactly when the swing would come, Danny slid his beer on to the bar and ducked. He stepped in behind the errant right of the big Irishman and landed two swift punches before sliding to the side and out of line with the left hook that was following the right that had found only air.

Both punches were precise, carefully calculated, delivered by rock-hard fists that landed with surprising force. Each opened a gash above one of McElroy's eyes. Blood instantly began to flow downward, blurring his vision. Danny stepped in behind McElroy's left hook that failed to connect. He delivered two swift blows to the bigger man's wind and slid away, avoiding a looping right.

McElroy swiped at his eyes in a vain effort to clear the blood from them so he could see. Even as he did, he howled in surprise and pain as one of Danny's boot heels smashed down with painful efficiency on the toes of one foot.

Instantly behind that surprising stab of pain, he felt his left ear flatten beneath the impact of a hard right hook from the young cowboy. It set his head to spinning and raised a roar in his head that confused and disoriented him.

Swiping in vain at the blood that was rendering his eyes useless, the big man felt his nose crushed by a straight left, then two teeth being knocked loose by a right that followed so closely behind it that it felt almost as if it were part of the same blow.

He staggered backward, helped along by a steady

9

rain of hammering blows that instantly turned his face to a shapeless mass of bleeding flesh. He shook his head, trying to clear away the red haze and unaccustomed confusion. He swung wildly with both fists, trying to find the opponent he had so badly underestimated.

Failing to connect with either hand, he spread his arms wide and lunged forward blindly, hoping to catch the smaller man in a bear hug, so he could use his superior size and strength. Instead he grasped only empty air. One foot was abruptly kicked out from under him, sending him reeling into the bar, striking the edge of it with the bridge of his nose. Three swift blows to the right side of his lower ribcage drove the breath from his lungs, accompanied by the snapping sound of at least one rib breaking.

He tried to lever himself away from the bar, but his hair was suddenly grasped in an iron grip. With the force of a triphammer, his face was slammed on to the plank that formed the top of the bar twice in rapid succession. Then, still with the steely grip on his hair, his head was jerked backward, sending him sprawling on to the rough planking of the floor.

He forced himself on to an elbow in a vain attempt to rise, then fell back again, too nearly unconscious to function.

The saloon, which had fallen silent in expectation of the young man's thrashing, erupted in a flurry of exclamations and comments. Because of that burst of activity and conversation nobody noticed a middle-aged cattleman walk into the bar and go directly to Hyatt. Those close enough heard his words, and they quickly became the dominant subject of conversation in Deadwood until the next saloon brawl or killing consigned them to oblivion. He said, 'Well, looks like you've had your recreation for the day, Danny.'

Danny grinned. 'Howdy, Dave. Just killin' time waitin' for you.'

The rancher snorted in response, obviously displeased but not surprised. 'Let's talk outside,' he said.

Danny shrugged. He quickly finished his beer and followed the older man outside. They walked to where five heavily armed men stood at obvious alert. 'I need you to take the saddle-bags that are on that packhorse and get them to Cheyenne.'

'What's in 'em?'

'Fifteen thousand dollars.'

Danny whistled. 'That's a lot of money. Why don't the guys you've got there take it?'

'Too obvious,' Dave Harrington replied. 'With that big an escort, it's obvious there's a lot of money there. That'll invite an ambush, sure's anything. If one man's just leading a packhorse, you'll look like any of a hundred idiots hopin' to strike it rich in the hills. That's why the pick an' shovel are tied on the pack.'

'Why me?'

Harrington looked him over appraisingly, reassuring himself of the decision he'd already

11

made. 'Because you're as good as any half a dozen men I could hire, and you can look like a hardscrabble nobody at the same time. If any man can get this to the bank in Cheyenne for me, it's you.'

'What's in it for me?'

'There's a thousand dollars waitin' for you at the bank in Cheyenne, when you turn the money over to 'em.'

Danny nodded with no apparent indication of surprise. 'Fair enough. You want me to leave right now?'

'The sooner the better.'

Not one of the group noticed the silent shadow between two of the clapboard buildings. The shadow didn't move for a long while, even after the rest had gone. Four hours later Danny was well on his way.

The night was quiet. It was two hours past dark. He knew a perfect spot to camp another hour further on. Then he'd be up at daylight, to make as much time as he could. Once out of the area, he could relax a little. He'd make his way on an erratic course through the Black Hills, pretending to stop and prospect regularly. The pick and shovel Harrington had added to the horse's pack were conspicuously tied where they would announce his identity as a prospector to anyone who bothered to glance at him. Once out of the Black Hills he would be beyond anyone who might be aware that he was working for a cattleman who had sold a very large herd of cattle at the boom town of Deadwood.

A full moon was just beginning to poke its nose

above the eastern horizon. It was just high enough to lend the softest of light now, but promised to bathe the land with clearer light imminently. Riding at a walk in the dark, Danny was fifty yards from a finger of timber when his horse's ears shot forward. The animal's head turned slightly, toward a spot in the trees.

With blurring speed, Danny's forty-five was in his hand, pointing in the direction the animal had indicated. He strained to pick out any movement in the deeper darkness of the trees. The night was so still he heard the soft click of a rifle hammer being cocked. He never even heard the shot.

CHAPTER 2

Donnelly's Saloon Number Six was as busy as usual. The long plank bar was lined with a combination of soldiers, prospectors and a few cowboys. A couple of them might have been homesteaders, from their dress.

The rest of the crude room was filled with tables. At one of them a spirited game of poker began to increase its stakes enough to interest spectators.

Five men sat around that table. One was slightly older than the others. His lined leathery face and calloused hands betokened a lifetime of hard work in the harsh sun and weather. The cigar he chewed as much as smoked indicated a level of prosperity well earned. He watched the other players with the practiced eye of a man with the ability to size up other men well and accurately.

The second player wore an army officer's uniform. He sat stiffly upright in his chair and spoke with military precision when making bets or conversation. Like the rancher, he studied the rest of the men at the table acutely.

The third and fourth players bore the look of drifters or prospectors. Their presence in the company of the others at poker suggested some measure of success in finding the elusive gold that had drawn so many to the Black Hills of Dakota. Neither appeared to be a very good poker player. Both played with the careless abandon of sudden wealth they thought inexhaustible.

The fifth player was entirely different in all respects. He looked as out of place there as an elephant in a cake social. The carefully tailored broadcloth suit displayed stark contrast with the coarse clothing of the rancher and the prospectors. He might have been a professional gambler, but something in his air belied that possibility as well. He spoke with well-polished English, with a slight but noticeable British accent. He was small and slender, perhaps five foot seven at most. He would have weighed no more than 140 pounds. His hands were small and soft, obviously unaccustomed to any sort of manual labor. He played with the slightest trace of a smile hovering always at the corners of his mouth, as if enjoying himself immensely but privately. Watching him, one might gather the impression he was more interested in the actions and reactions of the others at the table than in the pot itself.

As the evening had worn on, the stakes had grown appreciably higher. The winnings in front of the Englishman and the rancher were significantly greater than the other three. Easily more than a

$1,000 rested on the table top.

One of the prospectors, particularly, appeared on the verge of losing his way out of the game. Betting on the current hand had already been heavy. The prospector in question shoved all his remaining stake into the center of the table.

'I'll bet all I got left,' he declared.

The Englishman's eyebrows rose slightly, but he showed no other expression.

'Are you sure you want to do that?'

The prospector's headed thrust forward several inches immediately. 'Why wouldn't I?'

'You can't have that good a hand.'

'Why not? How do you know, anyway, unless these cards is marked or somethin'?'

The Englishman's expression didn't change. 'You took three cards in the draw, indicating that you had a pair, at best, at that time. I took only one. Mr Callahan took none, indicating a pat hand. Captain Winthrop took only one. Mr Bird folded. The numerical odds that you have a hand superior to the other three of us are extremely long. I would encourage you to reconsider that bet.'

'I don't need you tellin' me how to play poker.' The prospector bristled. 'You callin' or not?'

The Englishman gave an almost imperceptible shrug of his shoulders. 'You raised by fifty-three dollars, I believe,' he responded.

'My last fifty-three dollars,' the prospector agreed.

Miles Masters counted out fifty-three dollars and added them to the pot. 'If you won't heed the voice of reason, I will be forced to take the last of your money, I'm afraid. I call.'

Captain Winthrop tossed in his cards. 'The draw must've been better to you than it was to me.'

Ward Callahan studied Masters for a long moment. He counted out fifty-three dollars. 'I call.'

The prospector threw his cards triumphantly on to the table. 'Two pair! Kings an' sevens.'

Callahan laid his cards down. 'I'm afraid my nine high straight beats two pair.'

Masters smiled. 'I thought you might have a straight or a flush. I'm happy it was a straight. I believe my ace high straight is the superior hand.'

'Aaah!' the rancher said in disgust. 'I was sure I had you that time. You draw to an inside straight?'

'Oh my, no! I had the ten, jack, queen, king. I can't conceive of drawing to an inside straight. The odds would be only half as good that I might fill it.'

The all but forgotten prospector glared at the Englishman. 'You knowed. You knowed good an' well what the rest of us had. You wouldn'ta called me otherwise. You got them cards marked.'

'I would not stoop to playing with a marked deck,' Masters disagreed, careful to keep his voice calm and agreeable. 'If you remember, I did try to talk you out of betting the last of your money.'

'You're a cheat!' the prospector repeated.

With that he stood up from his chair, sending it crashing to the floor behind him. He clawed his gun from its holster.

Without appearing to move anything but his hand,

Masters whipped a .36 caliber Colt revolver from a shoulder holster beneath his suit coat. It barked twice in rapid succession.

The .45 of the prospector moved no further. Its rise to threaten the Englishman was halted by those two swift shots. Both bullets tore through his heart, rendering him lifeless before he hit the floor.

Masters sighed heavily, but gave no other expression. The Colt slid smoothly out of sight beneath his suit coat. He stood up and gathered the pot, along with his own stack of winnings from the table. 'Gentlemen, it would appear that this game has claimed a price too great for it to continue. I fear I must bid you cheerio.'

With that he strolled from the saloon as casually as if he had just finished a satisfying meal.

Only when he was out the door did the saloon come suddenly alive with a flurry of excited conversation.

CHAPTER 3

'Are you Cole Black?'

'No, just a little brown from the sun.'

Dave Harrington's taut face broke into an instant broad grin. 'By Jing, I guess I'd better get me some glasses, then.'

'That's usually a good idea for a fella your age,' came the instant rejoinder.

Harrington laughed aloud. 'That's two.'

'How many am I allowed?'

'Depends on my mood.'

'Maybe I'd better not push it then. What can I do for you?'

The older man thrust out a hand. 'My name's Dave Harrington.'

Cole frowned in thought as he returned the other's strong grip. 'Harrington. Sounds familiar. From the H-H Bar over toward the Big Horns?'

'That would be me.'

'Have a chair,' Black offered, waving to the empty chair on the other side of the small table.

19

'Thanks,' the other offered as he sat down. He laid his hat upside down on the floor beside the chair as he did so, and ran a hand across the thinning hair on top of his head.

'What can I do for you?' Cole repeated.

They were interrupted by the waitress in Cheyenne's Front Street café. 'You want dinner?'

'Yeah, I could stand that,' Harrington agreed. He looked across the table at Cole. 'You eat already?'

'Just fixin' to. It's on the way.'

'Coffee?' the waitress asked.

'Yeah. Thanks.'

'Busy place,' Harrington observed as she hurried away.

'Always is around noon,' Black agreed. 'Good food.'

Harrington opened his mouth to say something further, but was again interrupted. The waitress set two steaming cups of coffee before them and moved away. Both men picked up their respective cups and sipped the hot brew carefully. They had scarcely set them down again when the waitress returned with their food.

Neither man said anything then. Both devoted their full attention to devouring the food that had been set before them.

They were almost finished when Black glanced up at a nearby table. Just as he did, a big man sitting there reached out a hand and patted the waitress on the rear. She gave a small startled squeak as she whirled away from the man. The man laughed, leering at her.

Neither one saw Black move. He slid smoothly out of his chair, took one step, and landed a rock-hard fist squarely in the mouth of the man. The man flew from the chair that tipped over backward, and sprawled on to the floor. He came to rest against the leg of a chair at a nearby table. He rolled quickly to his hands and knees to rise, blood already spilling on to the café floor.

He didn't have time to stand, however. Cole leaned down, wrapped a burly left arm around the man's neck, and lifted him, firmly grasped in the headlock. As he did, his right fist smashed into the man's face again, landing with the sound of a broad hammer slamming into raw meat.

Cole never hesitated. He dragged the man, still firmly grasped in the headlock, toward the front door. With every step, his free fist slammed into the man's face again. By the time Cole heaved him out into the street, the man was unconscious. It was unlikely his face would ever have its previous contours again.

Black wiped his bloody hand on his trouser leg until it was reasonably clean. He returned to the café as if nothing had happened. He sat back down and ate the last few bites of his food. The two men who had been at the table with the victim of Cole's wrath slipped quietly from the table and headed for the door. He pretended not to notice either that, or the way Harrington quietly slid his .45 back into its holster.

When both had finished their meals the waitress reappeared. Trying not to look upset, she refilled their coffee cups. In spite of her best efforts, her hands trembled slightly. She picked up their empty plates, and started to walk away. Then she turned around. In a soft, tremulous voice she said, 'Thank you. Those three have been a terrible problem the past few days. The cook is afraid of them. He knew if he said anything to one of them, the other two would jump in too.'

'They thought some about it,' Harrington said. 'They sorta changed their minds.'

'I heard what you told them,' she said. She repeated, 'Thank you,' and hurried away.

Both men sipped their steaming coffee again. Black said, 'Thanks for backin' my play. I did notice you had your hogleg trained on them two.'

'Good of you to save me the trouble o' tendin' to that fella.'

Cole nodded. 'Seems like I said this before, some time or other, but what can I do for you?'

'Go to work for me.'

'Doin' what?'

'Find out who's killin' an' robbin' folks up around Deadwood.'

'That's a tall order. There's a gold rush goin' on up there. Gold draws the off-scouring of mankind like fresh cow chips draw flies.'

Harrington grinned. 'Off-scouring of mankind? I ain't heard that term for a goodly spell.'

Cole shrugged. 'Just popped into my head. What's

wrong with the law in Deadwood?'

It was Harrington's turn to shrug. 'There ain't a whole lot o' law in Deadwood. What there is, is too busy tryin' to keep up with fights an' shootin's in the saloons an' whorehouses. The town marshal's a good man, but he's just one man. There's a deputy United States marshal who's there off an' on, but he's kept busier than a hound dog scratchin' fleas tryin' to keep up with claim jumpers an' the like.'

'I'm sure that's true. Still and yet, it looks like robbery and murder ought to get their attention.'

'You'd think so, for sure. And mind you, I ain't sayin' that I think anyone wearin' a badge is involved in any way, but none of 'em seem any too eager to stop it. Maybe they just can't get any leads.'

'What's your stake in it?'

Harrington took a deep breath. 'Well, I sold a fine herd of steers and heifers there a while back. I was afraid of havin' trouble gettin' the money down to Cheyenne, here, to my bank. Like I said, there's been a rash of killin's and robberies lately. I hired the best man I ever knew to take the money to Cheyenne for me. Fifteen thousand dollars.'

Cole whistled at the amount, but said nothing.

Harrington continued. 'We made it up to look like he was just another hard-rock prospector wanderin' through the hills. He didn't make it five miles. Folks found him the next morning. He'd been shot from the timber, and robbed. Never had a chance. Never likely even seen whoever killed him.'

'How about your hands? They had to know you

had the money, and what you did with it.'

Harrington nodded. 'Several of 'em did. But the ones who did was with me the rest o' that night, an' still with me when someone rode into town the next day with news about the dead guy lyin' out there in the hills. It couldn'ta been any of my men. I'm plumb sure o' that.'

'And you want me to find out who did it?'

'And get my money back.'

'What's in it for me?'

'Name your price.'

Cole's eyebrows rose, but he offered no other expression. He took another drink of the coffee. 'Why'd you come to me?'

'I heard about the boys you chased down and taught the error of their ways down at Leadville. I figured if you could pull that off and ride away in one piece, you just might be able to deal with this one.'

'You did notice I ain't stickin' around anywhere close to Leadville any more?'

Dave Harrington nodded. 'That's part of what I heard. I heard you ain't the most popular fella with some of the powers that be down thataway.'

'I wasn't exactly offered the key to the city.' The big man grinned.

'But you got the job done.'

Cole nodded. 'I got the job done. Does a badge go with this deal?'

Dave shook his head. 'Not likely. Not unless we can wrangle a US deputy marshal's badge for you, and I ain't bettin' that'll happen. Like I said, there's

already one at Deadwood off an' on, and there ain't
a lot o' chance o' havin' two.'

'What help's available if I need it?'

'None. Not in a hurry, anyway. If you got time to
holler, me and the boys can ride over, but it'll take us
'bout three days at least to get there, ridin' hard.'

'You ain't exactly sugar-coatin' this thing, are you?'

'I wouldn't want a man to get the wrong idea. It
ain't gonna be easy.'

'How'd you know where to find me?'

'The boy that got killed asked me why I was hirin'
him instead of you. He knowed you was here in
Cheyenne.'

'Who was he?'

'Danny Hyatt.'

Cole's eyes widened. He stared hard at Dave for
fully half a minute. Eventually he breathed, 'Danny's
dead?'

Dave nodded glumly. 'He's the boy. I take it you
was friends. I didn't know that. I'm sorry.'

Cole nodded. 'He was like a kid brother to me. He
was with me at Leadville. I'd have been killed twice
up there if it wasn't for him. He was the only man I
ever met that I didn't think I could sure beat in a
stand-up fight.'

'He was one tough boy. If he run on to some guy
that was just plain mean, he'd pick a fight with him
every time, just for the sheer fun of takin' him down
a peg.'

'He was just as good with his guns. He could draw
and bust five bottles afore most men could get their

gun outa their holster.'

Dave nodded. 'I've seen 'im do it. Never did see 'im miss.'

'Neither did I. He was shot down from ambush, huh?'

'Never even saw it comin', I don't think.'

'What was you payin' 'im?'

'A thousand.'

Cole's eyes widened again. 'That's a lot of money for one trip from Deadwood to here.'

'It woulda been worth it, if he'd have made it.'

'Well, I'll take the thousand, if it's still on the table.'

'Fair enough. Do you want part of it now?'

'Nope. Only if and when I find out who did it and take care of him. Or them.'

'The thousand's enough?'

'The thousand's a-plenty. I'd do it for nothin'. Just for Danny. I'll be there day after tomorrow.'

Dave left Cheyenne feeling that he had probably done the best he could do. Or the worst. He didn't admit to the feeling that his best probably wouldn't be good enough. The worst was that he might have simply sent a second man to his death.

CHAPTER 4

Coleman Black could never have explained why he turned aside, just there. His way lay following the creek that babbled happily along the bottom of the wide draw. He wasn't in gold country yet, so the water was still clear as crystal. He'd already decided he'd fish a trout out of one of its pools for supper.

The hills were thick with northern pines, cedars and occasional spruce, stretching tall, reaching high for their share of sunlight. In the clearer spaces, the leaves of aspen trees quivered in the light breeze. An occasional cottonwood spread its broad branches where the water was more plentiful. The white undersides of their leaves created an almost aspen-like effect when a breeze lifted or turned them. It was as close to idyllic as any place in the Black Hills of Dakota Territory would be for many years to come.

Further north, the rapacious furor of gold fever had already ripped apart the fabric of the hills, turned the creeks to mud, destroyed much of the

27

vegetation, and nearly all the wildlife. Cole had spent a year in Leadville, Colorado, where the same thing had happened at the headwaters of the Arkansas River. He almost shuddered, knowing what was coming here as well. What gold did to a country took generations to heal. What it did to men often never did.

Even as he thrust that thought away, he noticed the broad, flat-bottomed gulch opening up along the right-hand side of the valley he followed. There was no reason for it to spark his interest. It was no different from a hundred other small gulches and valleys opening back deeper into the hills. Even so, it seemed as if some unseen magnet reached out from there, calling to him, drawing him by some gossamer strand that belonged to a different dimension.

He frowned as the unprecedented feeling tingled along his spine. He reined in his horse and stared in that direction. A couple blue jays, still out of sight around a bend of the gulch, squawked loud protests at something disturbing them. Beyond that, there was no indication of anything to attract his attention. There was nothing in his experience to explain the persistent feeling.

Still, something had jerked his mind in that direction as if pulled by a cobweb leash. He knew himself well enough to know he'd fret over it for days if he failed to follow his instincts. He reined his big, deep-chested, chestnut gelding around and skirted the hogback that marked the beginning of the lesser gulch. Almost as soon as he did, he could hear faint sounds coming from a copse of hardwood trees.

He slid from the saddle and dropped the reins to the ground, knowing the gelding would stand indefinitely without being tethered. He crept soundlessly from brush to tree to the next clump of brush, keeping as much vegetation as possible between himself and the meager sounds that guided him. Without realizing he had even reached for it, his Colt .45 was in his hand.

It took him ten minutes to navigate unseen to the small clearing whose activities had somehow reached out unseen tentacles to summon him. He didn't understand such things, but had long since learned to trust his instincts about them, and so had approached cautiously.

At the far side of the clearing a great cottonwood spread its massive branches over a broad area. Beneath one of those branches, a raggedly dressed black man was seated bareback on an old and bony mare that had to be all of thirty years old. A worn flop hat lay on the ground beside them. The man's hands were firmly tied behind him. The loop of a lariat was snugged around his neck, with the rope run up over a limb of the cottonwood. Another man was busily tying the loose end to the tree trunk.

Ranged around the one about to be hung were three other men. Two of them wore trousers that represented what was left of Confederate uniforms. 'You shoulda run from that ridge when you had the chance clear back there,' one of them declared.

The black man shook his head in obvious

29

desperation. 'I wasn't never nowheres near Cemetery Ridge, suhs. I didn't fight in that war nowheres. I just only got freed when it was all over.'

'You sure look like the nigger that shot my brother in the back that day,' another of the men declared. 'Even if you ain't, you'll do just as well. There ain't no room out here in this country for niggers nohow.'

The black man's eyes were huge white orbs in the dark of his face. Fear and despair took turns passing across his expression. His voice was plaintive. 'I ain't done nothin' to get hunged for,' he insisted.

'Ain't no sense arguin' with a nigger,' one of the riders asserted. 'Just do it.'

'He's had long enough to jabber an' beg,' another agreed.

'You cain't just hang a man for nothin',' the black man insisted.

'You're a nigger. That's enough,' another of the mounted men asserted.

The black man opened his mouth again, as if to further plead his case. He cast a searching look around the half-circle of his executioners. Two of the mounted men glared in undisguised hatred. The third man grinned in unrestrained glee and anticipation. Seeing neither mercy nor reason in their faces, the black man simply closed his mouth. He nodded once, in stoic acceptance of his fate. 'Well, then, I guess y'all had just as well get it done with,' he conceded.

The one who had tied up the loose end of the lariat-become-hangman's-noose walked over and slapped the old nag on the rump. She humped her back momentarily, but failed to run out from under her owner. She tossed her head once, as if to telegraph refusal to be the instrument of his death.

One of the mounted men swore. He rode forward, shaking out his own lariat. He swung a length of it, whipping it viciously across the old mare's rump, as he yelled at the top of his voice. This time the horse lunged forward, and the black man slid across her back, into the empty void that would plunge him to the end of the rope.

The dreaded constriction of his throat failed to occur, however. Instead an unexpected shot rang out. The rope, just where it crossed the branch above his head, parted. He landed with a thump on the ground, his hands still tied, the loop still around his neck.

One of the mounted men was possessed of incredibly quick reflexes. His gun leaped into his hand instantly, already turned toward the sound of that surprise shot. Coleman Black's reflexes were just as quick. Before the rider could fire, a second shot from Cole's pistol knocked him from his saddle.

The other three men clawed for their weapons as if on a single command. Several shots, too closely spaced amongst their own echoes that bounced off the walls of the narrow gulch to count, created a momentary roar of sound that beat physically against the ears of the wide-eyed black man seated helplessly on the ground.

Sudden silence replaced the surfeit of explosive

31

noise. As if standing in a secure and placid target range, Coleman Black expended five empty casings from his Colt .45. He replaced them with fresh cartridges. Even as he did, his eyes darted from one supine figure to the next, watching for any indication of residual danger.

When he had finished reloading, he kept his gun in hand as he walked from one to the other of the would-be lynchers. None showed any signs of life. Even so, he carefully removed their weapons and gun belts, even checking them for hideout weapons as well. Two of the four did, indeed, have such back-up arms.

Only then did he walk to the black man. Wordlessly he slid a large knife from its sheath at his belt. At the touch of the blade, the ropes binding the man's wrists together parted and fell away.

As if the action released some hidden spring within him, the man leaped to his feet. He grasped the rope around his neck. Loosening the loop, he jerked it over his head, and threw it as far from him as he could. He stood there, trembling, staring at the lifeless piece of hemp as if it were some great evil upon which his fear and anger could focus.

After a full minute, he relaxed perceptibly. He turned to face his rescuer. 'Suh, I don't know who you are, 'ceptin' maybe a rescuin' angel o' God, but I is much awful obliged to y'all. I shore thunk my days was ended. I could pertneart hear that angel choir a-singin'. I thought I was as dead as Abel, an' there was four sons o' Cain makin' sure of it.'

Cole chuckled in spite of the severity of the situation. 'What's your name?' he asked.

The black man stopped the gushing flow of words and took a deep breath. He stood up straighter and squared his shoulders. He looked full into Cole's face for the first time. 'Suh, my name is Revelation Sword White, so named by a mother what told me I was destined to be a sword for right and justice in the land.'

Cole chuckled again. 'Well, now, that's somethin', that is.'

'What's y'all mean?'

'My name is Coleman Black.'

Revelation Sword White stared uncomprehendingly at him. 'Suh, I doesn't see what's funny 'bout that there.'

Cole grinned in response. 'Think about it. I'm Coleman Black. You're Revelation White. I'm Black. You're White.'

The irony of the coincidence struck the rescued man at last. He opened his mouth wide, tipping his head back and laughing uproariously. He slapped his thigh. 'That's a sign from the Lord, just as shore as shore can be,' he declared. 'That's somethin' that ain't never gonna happen twice 'twixt now an' when the Lord comes!'

'Where you headin'?' Cole interrupted the rapid, excited flow of the man's words.

'Well, suh, I ain't just rightly sure. I was sorta headin' towards that Deadwood place. I figured as how in a place overrun with folks, like I heard it is, there'd be a job or two what nobody else wanted that a freed slave could take on, just to keep body and soul together.'

'I 'spect there is,' Cole agreed. 'What do you go by?'

'My name, suh, is Revelation Sword White—'

Cole interrupted. 'Yeah, I know. You told me that. But that's quite a mouthful. What do folks call you when they don't want to spit out a handle that long?'

White looked at Cole in silence for quite a bit. Then he said, 'Well, suh, mostly I was just called "Boy" for most of my life. But I don't really like that there. When I was freed, I figured as how I didn't never need to answer to "Boy" ever again.'

'I can understand that,' Cole affirmed. 'But what did your own kind call you?'

Again the man studied him carefully before he answered. 'Well, suh, mostly they called me Gideon.'

'Gideon?'

'Gideon.'

'Where did they get Gideon out of Revelation Sword White?'

He shrugged. 'I ain't just right shore, Suh, but I 'spect as how maybe it's on account o' Gideon a-havin' everyone holler, "The sword of the Lord and of Gideon," so they done connected the sword in my name with him.'

'Well, Gideon's a lot easier to spit out than the other, so if you don't mind I'll just call you Gideon.'

'Yes, suh, mista Black. That there'll be just fine.'

'As long as you don't call me "mister" or "sir",'

34

Cole corrected.

Gideon frowned. 'Well, suh—'

'Cole.'

'What?'

'Cole.'

'Cole what, suh?'

'Not sir. Just Cole. My name's Cole. Just call me Cole.'

Gideon opened his mouth twice as if to protest, and closed it each time. He frowned as he wrapped his mind around a concept obviously new and strange to him. Never in his life had he dared to call a white man by his first name. It would not come easily, but he suddenly liked the idea. He suddenly liked that idea a lot.

'Cole,' he repeated with a broad and toothy grin. 'Well, uh, Cole, I surely do thank y'all for a-savin' my scrawny black neck this day.'

'It sorta looked like it could use some savin'.' Cole grinned.

'It surely did, su . . . uh, Cole,' he agreed.

'So now what?' Cole queried.

Gideon frowned and shook his head. 'I don't rightly know, su . . . uh, Cole. Like I done said, I was fixin' to head up to Deadwood. . . .'

'That's where I'm headed,' Cole offered. 'If you'd like, you can team up with me and we'll ride together.'

'Well, now, that there's an offer I ain't never contemplated afore. I'd be plumb proud to ride along with you . . . Cole.'

Cole glanced around at the quartet of dead men. 'We seem to have some business to take care of here, first.'

'We do gotta bury all these here dead men,' Gideon agreed.

'That we do,' Cole agreed. 'Then there's the matter of their stuff. Do you own a gun?'

'No, suh.'

'Cole.'

'Uh, no . . . Cole.'

'You don't own a saddle either, apparently?'

'No . . . uh, no.'

'Do you have any money?'

'I has three dollars and seven cents.'

'Not exactly a big stake.'

'Why is you askin' me all this?'

Cole frowned thoughtfully. 'Well, it seems to me these four have a lot of the stuff you sure need. They intended, and tried, to take your life. They don't need a bit of it any more. It seems to me it'd be just and right for them to outfit you with a good horse and saddle, a bedroll, a couple or three guns and ammunition, and whatever money they happen to be carryin'.'

'I'm a poor man,' Gideon protested, 'but I ain't poor enough to go robbin' the dead. That there just don't seem like it'd be seemly atall.'

Cole thought for a long moment before he answered. Then he said, 'Well, you've obviously been taught some about the things in the Bible.'

'Yes su . . . I mean, uh, yes. I knows the Good Book right well.'

'Well, back then, when there was a battle, wasn't it the right and proper thing for the ones that won the battle to have the spoils of war?'

Understanding spread across Gideon's face as it opened up into a huge display of gleaming white teeth. 'Why, I didn't never think of it like that there.'

Almost as swiftly his face fell. 'But I ain't the one what won no battles. You the one did that. I just sat there on the ground with my hands tied an' my mouth open a-watchin'.'

'Doesn't matter,' Cole argued. 'That just means I get first pick, and you get to pick whatever you want after.'

Gideon's eyes darted around the prostrate bodies, then at their horses. One in particular was a fine mare of obvious strength and breeding. Her saddle and bridle were far superior to the others. She bore no brand. 'That one there's a mighty fine horse,' he observed.

'Then I'd say it's yours,' Cole said. 'You might want to go through the stuff in the saddle-bags and bedroll, and get rid of anything with his name on it. He's got the best guns of any of them as well.'

'We'd best be givin' these men as good a Christian burial as we can first,' Gideon protested. 'I'll do the diggin'. Then I'd shore 'nough like to move on from here a ways afore we camp for the night. Then I can show you how good I can catch us some fish for supper an' cook 'em up good enough to make your mouth water for a week just rememberin' how good they was.'

'You got a shovel?'

Gideon's face fell once again. His eyes darted around the clearing again. 'Right there! There's a short shovel on that horse right over there.'

Cole glanced that way, confirming Gideon's observation. 'One good thing about gold fever,' he observed. 'One of them thought to bring along a shovel.'

CHAPTER 5

Revelation Sword White was as good as his word. He caught four large trout from the stream that babbled through the long valley. He cooked them, fried potatoes that Cole furnished from his pack, and made biscuits in a Dutch oven, so light and fluffy they threatened to float away on the breeze. When he had eaten until his stomach hurt, Cole laid back against his still-rolled-up bedroll. 'Where'd you learn to cook like that, Gideon?'

'That's what I done, in the Whites' house,' he explained. 'I been cookin' since I was knee-high to a grasshopper.'

'It shows. Can you use those guns?'

Self-consciously Gideon's hand brushed the unfamiliar gun tied low on his hip, where Cole had instructed it to be placed. 'No suh. I mean, Cole. I's good with a scattergun, 'cause it was up to me to shoot quail an' partridge an' such when Mistah White wanted 'em for supper some days. But I ain't never shot a handgun like this here afore.'

Cole unfolded himself from the ground. 'Well, we'd best commence to teachin' you how, then. There ain't many things more dangerous than packin' a gun that ain't loaded, or one that you can't use.'

'I'd shore be much obliged if 'n you was to show me,' Gideon agreed.

In the hour that followed Cole instructed the eager student on the workings, cleaning, care and use of the .45 caliber revolver. He taught him how to place his thumb crosswise across the hammer as he drew, thumbing the hammer back in the same motion as he lifted the gun, releasing the hammer and squeezing the trigger at the precise instant the gun came level.

'That's one of the things you have to learn if you want to stay alive,' Cole lectured. 'Don't ever draw unless you're sure you're going to shoot. And don't ever draw without shooting at the instant your gun comes level. If you hesitate, even a heartbeat, before you squeeze the trigger, you'll be a dead man. It has to all be one instinctive motion, from the time you grab the gun.'

They practiced it until Gideon's arm felt as if it would drop off. Slowly, to get all the moves right, over and over and over. When the moves were right, Cole had him load the weapon, and begin firing it as it came level. In a surprisingly short time the motion became fluid and smooth, and the bullets began to strike closer and closer to their mark.

When darkness ended the lessons, he made sure

Gideon cleaned the gun thoroughly, oiled it well, then wiped away all traces of the oil. Then he made sure Gideon had loaded it properly, and secured it back in its holster. 'We'll work on it every day,' Cole promised. 'After we get to Deadwood, you need to keep working on it. Every day. If you can't get out of town somewhere that you can shoot, just practice drawing and shooting without any ammunition in it. If you do that at least fifty times every day, you'll be good enough to use it when you need it.'

Cole kept his word to continue the lessons until they got to their destination. Because of the time spent doing so, it took the pair three more days to make their way to Deadwood. They also developed a surprising and close friendship.

As they prepared for the last day's short ride into the boom town, Cole said, 'You might want to put the gun in your bedroll when we ride into town. A black man packin' that good a gun might be a challenge to some men.'

Gideon nodded in agreement. 'I's already thought mighty hard on that, Cole,' he replied, at last saying the white man's name without hesitation. 'I 'spect as how they's other black folks already in Deadwood. I sorta thought I'd either be your "boy" onest we hit town, or else I'd ask you to hang on to my stuff for me, and I'll see if 'n I can find me a job somewheres.'

Cole pursed his lips thoughtfully before answering. 'I'd like havin' you with me, but it might cause more problems than help,' he conjectured. 'It'd probably be better for you to find a job and a place to live, but find a way to keep in touch with me. I'll hang on to your stuff, though, if you want me to.'

Just over a ridge from the first outreaches of the sprawling mining camp, Gideon selected the things he would keep in a gunny sack slung over his shoulder. He walked into Deadwood, looking for all the world like a half-starved, friendless ex-slave, living on the edge of desperation. Nobody would have suspected he carried $375 in his ragged corduroy trousers.

An hour later Cole rode into town leading a riderless horse, and put both animals up at the first livery barn he came to.

The next day, riding Gideon's mare, he rode out to find the site of the murder he had been hired to investigate. From the rancher's description, he found it swiftly. He could see the blackened earth where his friend's lifeblood had stained the ground. It was late summer, and it seldom rained during the late months of summer. There hadn't been nearly sufficient precipitation to eradicate the unmistakably dark patch of ground.

He squatted there, touching the preternaturally dark earth, as if he might be able to feel there the pulse that had faded and stopped as the young man died. Or as if those stains in the soil could speak to him of who had lain in wait to end his life. A long-forgotten phrase popped into his mind: *Your brother's blood cries out to me from the ground.*

He stood with a heavy sigh. Looking around, he quickly picked out the likely spot from which the killer had awaited his quarry. He mounted and rode the fifty yards to a finger of timber, and dismounted. Walking into the timber, he swiftly found a spot where the earth had obviously been disturbed. He frowned as he studied it.

All the usual debris of a forest floor was either missing or lying in unnatural ways. It looked as if somebody had taken a broom and swept it back and forth, obliterating all marks it might have held. Following the trail of that sweeping, Cole walked back deep into the timber, then to one side. Some distance from the edge of the timber there, the ground showed evidence of a horse's arrival and departure. No hoofprints were visible, but enough grass had been broken and trampled to reveal the direction from which it had come, and to which it returned.

Cole swore. 'Wiped out anything that'd make him easy to identify,' he muttered. 'Didn't make any effort to make it look natural. Just swept away anything that could be recognized. Whatd'ya bet, if I follow them tracks, they'll end up on hard ground or rock?'

He followed them anyway, until he had established that that was, indeed, the fact. The trail of brushed-away tracks ended at an expanse of windswept rocks that would reveal no history of who or what had walked on their unyielding surface. Men or animals of many stripes might have walked there recently, or thousands of years before. It was all the same to the changeless rock. It would reveal the secrets of

43

neither. Nothing would be found at the scene to identify Danny's killer.

Cole summarized his findings. 'Well, whoever it was knew he had the money. He wasn't just sitting there in the timber to see who might happen along. He figured out what direction Danny was going to go, so he knew where to wait for him. Then he shot him down in cold blood, without even a warning. He left his horse tied where it was, walked to the body, took the money, walked back to his horse, wiping out all his tracks, and just rode away. Cold-blooded as a sidewinder.'

He shuddered slightly, thinking about a human being capable of acting in such a manner. The task he had accepted was not going to be easy. The chill that crawled up his spine assured him it might even prove fatal for him.

CHAPTER 6

It was not what he expected when he opened the door. If all of life's surprises were that pleasant, he'd gladly opt to live forever.

Cole rented a room at the first hotel he found, then walked to the office of the town marshal. It seemed the appropriate place to start. When he opened the door and walked in, his eyes lit on the most beautiful woman he had ever seen. He stood there, mouth agape, staring.

She smiled, and his world lit up more brightly than if the sun had taken up residence in Deadwood. He swept the hat from his head, half-returning the smile, but simultaneously feeling grimy and unkempt from the trail.

'Can I help you?' she asked.

Her voice was as musical as her face was magical. He felt suddenly as if he had been transported into some fairy tale and confronted there by a mythical princess. He certainly didn't feel like any Prince Charming, though. He felt suddenly crude, dirty, and out of place.

'Uh, I, uh, I'm, uh, I'm sorry. I thought this was the marshal's office.'

Her smile broadened. Her voice was bright and chipper. 'Oh, you're right. It is.'

He frowned in total incomprehension. 'You, uh, you ain't, uh, aren't, I mean. . . .'

She laughed brightly, obviously enjoying his discomfiture. 'No, I'm certainly not the marshal. I'm his daughter. I take care of a lot of the paperwork for him, and mind the office when he has to be gone. Now, how can I help you?'

Cole took a deep breath. 'Well, you could maybe just sit there and let me stare with my mouth hanging open a little longer, then I'll go back out and come back in again, and see if I can act and sound less like the village idiot next time.'

She laughed again, and he thought it was the most beautiful music he had ever heard. 'That won't be necessary. I understand it was a bit startling to find me here instead of Father.'

He grinned more easily. 'More than a bit. I'm Cole Black.'

'You don't look that dark to me.'

'That's my favorite line!' he protested. 'When folks ask me if I'm Cole Black I usually say I'm just dark from the sun.'

She giggled as if she hadn't already made use of the oddity of his name herself. 'And what would you say if the other man said, 'I'm Al White.'

His grin broadened. 'Strange you should say that!

I just met a fellow a few days ago that is about the blackest Negro I've ever seen. His last name, believe it or not, is White. We rode together for a ways. We got a big kick out of arguing which one was white and which was black.'

'Oh, that's just too funny,' she agreed. 'I'm Martha McLauren.'

'Martha McLauren,' he repeated, 'with the bluest eyes and the prettiest red hair this side of heaven.'

He was rewarded with a pink flush that rushed up her face, making it even more breathtakingly beautiful than before. 'Oooh, and he's a smooth talker, too,' she taunted.

'To tell the truth, I've never really wanted to be until just this minute,' he countered. 'Right now, I sure wish I knew all the witty and fetching things a man's supposed to say.'

'You're not doing too badly, if you really want to know,' she rejoined. 'Now, at the risk of sounding terribly repetitious, what can I do for you?'

He forced himself to stop staring at her captivating beauty and remember his reason for being there. 'Well, I'm looking for information.'

'What kind of information?'

'I'm wondering if the marshal . . . uh, your father . . . has any information about who might be the one behind the robberies going on lately?'

Her posture and expression changed instantly. Her eyes clouded. Her brow lowered. Her jaw set. Tiny, half-circle lines appeared at the corners of her mouth. She shook her head. 'He's as mystified as everybody else, and it's driving him crazy,' she said. 'There are a lot of robberies all the time, it seems like, but these are different. It's always people who have a lot of money, or a lot of gold, and they're just killed. Executed. Just shot down in cold blood, with no chance to even give up the money to save their life or anything.'

Then, as if a totally new thought had intruded itself, she stared hard at him. 'Why? What does all that have to do with you?'

He started to tell her he was hired by Dave Harrington, then suddenly didn't want to tell her that. He didn't want her to think he was a hired gun, concerned only because he stood to make a lot of money if he could solve the mystery. He didn't know why. There was nothing either dishonest or dishonorable about his motives or his situation. He just wanted her to think of him more highly than as of a mercenary gunman.

'Do you remember a young guy named Danny Hyatt?'

She nodded, the pained look still in her eyes. 'He's the really nice young man who was carrying all the money from the sale of some rancher's cattle.'

Cole nodded. 'He was a mighty close friend of mine, like a brother to me. Dave Harrington, the man he was working for, rode clear to Cheyenne to let me know about it. He asked me to try to find out who killed Danny. I'd have come even if he didn't ask, though.'

'Are you a lawman?'

He shook his head. 'Not just now. I've been a deputy US marshal twice. So was Danny when we worked together in Colorado, up in mining country there.'

'I see. Then you should talk with Father. I'm sure he will want to talk with you.'

'Does he have any ideas?'

She hesitated a long while before she answered. 'I think you'd best talk with him. I don't want to be telling stories out of school.'

His estimation of her went up several notches with her words. 'When would I have a chance to talk with him, then?'

'Not for a few days. He's out of town on business for a few days. When he gets back, I'll tell him you'd like to talk with him. Are you staying in town?'

He nodded. 'I'm staying at the Deadwood Hotel. It had the most imaginative name I could find.'

She rewarded the witticism with a giggle. 'A little pretentious, but not bad,' she agreed. 'At least they didn't call it a palace or something.'

He left, already thinking of half a dozen excuses that would bring him back to the town marshal's office in the coming days.

CHAPTER 7

The soft rapping at his door sent Cole out of the covers, gun in hand. 'Who's there?'

'It's me, su . . . uh, Cole,' Gideon's unmistakable accent responded. Cole grinned, lowering the gun. 'Just a second.'

He removed the straight-back chair that was propped beneath the doorknob and opened the door. The black man slid through the door and closed it quickly behind him. Cole noticed with surprise the .45 Gideon was wearing, but said nothing about it. 'What's up?' he queried.

'I didn't want nobody to see me comin' here,' Gideon offered, instead of answering. 'I thought maybe I'd be better bein' your ears here an' there if nobody figured out we knowed one another. That's why I's here so early, afore it's light.'

'That makes sense,' Cole commended. 'I could sure use an extra pair of ears. This isn't going to be an easy thing to solve.'

Gideon nodded rapidly. 'That's how come I's here.

I's plumb scared there's gonna be another one o' them killin's afore the day's done.'

Cole frowned. 'Who? Why?'

Gideon's eyes cast swiftly around the room, as if searching for hidden listeners. 'I's got me a job.'

'Good! That didn't take you very long.'

'Oh, no suh. There's jobs to be had all over Deadwood, if 'n you ain't fussy 'bout what you gotta do. I's got a job a-cleanin' up Number Six. I's got a room in the back to live in, and I's got to clean up the saloon after everyone's done gone. That's what I just got done a-doin'. Then, later on when they's all up an' outa bed, I gotta clean up all the girls's rooms too. Them harlot girls, you know.'

'I always wondered if they did their own housework,' Cole admitted.

'No suh. That there's my job now. At Number Six, that is. The best part is, I gets to smell all them perfumes they keep on their dressers. Don't hurt none to smell 'em, you know. They sure do smell good. There's two o' them what's black, too. Sally an' Milly. Millicent.'

'I'm sure that's not what you came to tell me.'

'Oh, no suh. Uh, I mean, Cole. I done comed over here to let you know that there's a fella what just might be about to get hisself shot, just like your friend done.'

'Who? Why?' Cole asked again.

'Well, his name is Duck. At least, that's what folks calls him. I done some askin', what I could without actin' like I'd done forgot my place. His name's really

51

Farnsworth Duckett.'

Cole shook his head. 'I haven't heard the name.'

'He be one o' them ranch fellas. Cattle ranch fella. He be havin' a ranch some ways west o' Deadwood.'

'Why is somebody likely to kill him?'

'Money. He done won a whole lot o' money.'

'At Number Six?'

Gideon, nodded his head emphatically. 'Playin' poker, they was. They was gamblin' some big money. It was big enough everybody in the place was crowded around a-watchin'. Some folks was even bettin' on who was gonna be the biggest winners. Well, this Mister Duck fella, he was the one that won pertneart all the money on the table. They was more money there than I's ever seed all in one place.'

'He really cleaned house, huh?'

'Oh, he sure done that. He cleaned house an' pockets both, cleaner'n a new whistle.'

'Then what happened?'

'Well, he bought everyone in Number Six a drink. All the harlots in the place was makin' up to him somethin' shameless, whisperin' stuff in his ear an' all, but he wasn't havin' nothin' to do with them.'

'Well, that says something for him.'

'There was three or four fellas what offered to leave with him then. They said they'd ride all the way to his ranch with him, to make sure someone didn't go hittin' him over the head to get all that money.'

'Did he know the guys?'

'Yessuh. He seemed to know 'em all right enough. Called 'em by name. Thanked 'em plumb polite-like.

52

He done tol' 'em he'd hole up here in this here hotel, an' stick a chair under the doorknob. Then he'd ride home today, when it's good an' daylight. He's plumb awful sure there ain't nobody gonna try to rob him in broad daylight.'

Cole glanced at the window. The early rays of dawn already streaked the eastern sky with swaths of pink and gold. He swore under his breath.

'I'll see if I can head him off, or at least ride with him,' he declared.

'I was figgerin' you'd do that there,' Gideon agreed. 'He most likely won't be waitin' too late to start, even if he was up half the night a-gamblin' an' drinkin'.'

'Can you get away to ride with me?'

Gideon nodded, grinning broadly. 'I was hopin' y'all might ask. I left word that I was feelin' peaked, and was headin' down to shanty town to have Ma Jones fix me up with some medicine. I done saddled both our horses and brunged 'em around. They's tied up out o' sight, out back, at the edge o' the cliff. I'll head back out there an' wait for you.'

Gideon opened the door and looked cautiously both ways before he slipped into the hall and scurried swiftly to the back stairs. Cole propped the door shut again, dressed hurriedly, and left.

At the desk he asked the clerk, 'Did Mr Duckworth already leave?'

The clerk nodded. 'You missed him by almost an hour.'

Cursing again to himself, Cole hurried to the spot

53

where Gideon waited with the horses. 'Do you know where this Duckworth's place is?'

'Yes suh. I mean, Cole. I asked the night hostler at the livery barn what's the quickest way to Duckworth's spread.'

'He was willing to tell you?'

'He didn't have no problem with it. Especially when he seed the gun I was wearin'. I ain't never seed a white man look at me with that kind o' respect afore. I plumb liked that feelin'. I's sorta wonderin' if I wanta go back to bein' a saloon swamper when we get back. O' course, if'n I doesn't, I ain't rightly sure how I'd make a livin', though.'

Cole's voice bore the barest trace of impatience. 'So what's the way to the ranch?'

Brought back from his musings, Gideon responded, 'Mista Duck's? Just foller the main road straight west, the man said. As soon as we get past the crick, take the first trail that forks off to the left. That one'll lead you straight to it.'

'Did he say how far it is?'

'Upwards o' fifteen, sixteen miles, he say. He say it seems like more, 'cause most o' the way's through the hills.'

'Then let's get movin',' Cole muttered as he swung into the saddle.

They rode at a swift canter for the first mile and a half, then slowed to a swift, ground-eating trot. They swung off the main road on to the trail the hostler had indicated. Cole noted with satisfaction the fresh trail of a single horse ahead of them.

'Well, he's gotten away from town at least. Nobody seems to be following him. He just might make it,' he suggested.

They were two miles further down the road before his optimism was shattered. Topping a small rise he spotted a single horse, standing in the middle of the trail. Almost as swiftly, he spotted the dark lump on the ground beside it.

Even though he knew instantly that he was too late to do anything helpful, he clamped the spurs to the gelding's sides. The animal responded instantly, lunging forward, then settling into a smooth running gait. The ground beneath them swept to a blur. Cole's hat brim blew up tightly against the crown of his hat, but he stayed erect in the saddle. His eyes constantly scanned the country around and ahead of him.

He slid the gelding to a stop and leaped from the saddle. He turned the rancher over, noticing as he did the large bloody hole in his back. He knew from that that the bullet that felled him had passed clear through his chest. Against all odds, the man was still alive.

'Duck?' Cole demanded. 'Who shot you?'

The rancher gathered his rapidly waning strength in a valiant effort to speak. 'Didn't even see. . . .'

His strength ebbed away without his being able to complete the sentence. He didn't need to. Cole had heard exactly what he had feared.

Didn't even see. . . .

Didn't even see his killer. Didn't have any warning.

Didn't know he had only minutes to live, until the bullet tore through his flesh and knocked him from the saddle.

The contents of the rancher's saddle-bags and bedroll were strewn around on the ground. There was no money to be found.

Cole looked again at the wound that had felled the hapless rancher. He pictured him riding his horse along the trail, and calculated immediately the direction from which the shot had come. A large outcropping of rocks jutted skyward about seventy-five yards away.

He pointed in that direction. 'Shot came from over there,' he said.

Gideon sat his horse, looking for all the world as if he were responsible for the rancher's death. 'I done waited too long,' he lamented. 'I done waited too long.'

Without answering, Cole mounted the gelding and trotted to the rocks. He dismounted and climbed around in them until he found where the gunman had waited. Matted grass and packed ground indicated the spot, just behind a rock that would have provided a perfect rest for a patient rifle.

He worked back through the rocks, looking for tracks. Every place where the ground was soft enough to leave any kind of print had been swept clean by a brushy branch of evergreen. Pine needles knocked from the shrubs in the process lay here and there out of place.

He followed the brushed-away trail to a broad

expanse of hard shale that led off to the north as far as he could see. 'He'll follow that all the way back across to the main road,' Cole hypothesized, 'then his tracks will be impossible to pick out from all the others.' He swore under his breath.

'Can you read sign like that there?' Gideon asked.

'I can if there's any sign to read,' Cole bit the words short. 'This guy uses a tree branch to wipe away anything that I could use to tell who he is.'

Frustration churning in his gut, he returned to the rancher. He gathered the man's belongings and secured them into his saddle-bags and bedroll. Then, with Gideon's welcome help, he heaved the man himself across the saddle, tying him into place with the ever-present lariat tied to the pommel.

After several minutes of consideration, he decided to take the man home instead of back to Deadwood. That would mean he would have to face the man's family, if he had family. Or his crew, at the very least. Even so, it was better than just dumping him off back in the bustle of a boom town too busy to even notice his passing. At least at his spread, the folks would care that he had been killed. He would be grieved for. Somehow, he thought he'd like it better that way.

He instructed Gideon to return to Deadwood and keep his ears open. Then he started the trek he wanted not to have to make.

CHAPTER 8

It was late by the time Cole returned the slain rancher to his home. He would rather have taken a beating than have to bring the dead man to his wife, his family, his crew. Their shock and grief ran deep. All of them knew their lives would never be the same. Because it fell to his lot to bring the unwelcome news and the man's body, he felt as if he were, somehow, responsible for their grief and pain.

Cole accepted the invitation to spend the night in the bunkhouse. This morning he had left before daylight, determined to talk to prospectors with a claim in the area, homesteaders, anybody in the area of the man's murder who might have heard or seen something.

That was why he happened to follow the path to the place he now eyed from the top of a low knoll.

The homesteader's shack was as ramshackle as any Cole had seen. It had been cobbled together with odds and ends of almost everything imaginable. Its lone window was oddly shaped, apparently made to fit the broken piece of glass that filled it.

A steel-gray gelding grazed a hundred yards from the house, his front feet hobbled to keep him close and easy to catch. He, at least, was in better shape than any other living thing in sight.

The yard was almost completely barren of vegetation. Several chickens scratched for sustenance well away from the yard. Closer, on the other side of the yard, a hoghouse and accompanying pen emitted grunts and squeals testifying to the presence of their occupants.

What passed for a cowshed behind the house had a door that hung crookedly from one hinge. It appeared to be empty. If the place boasted a cow or two, they were scrounging for grass some place other than near the shed.

Altogether it was the sorriest-looking domicile Cole could ever remember seeing. Every detail of the place echoed a desperate level of both neglect and poverty.

The homesteader himself was every bit as abject in appearance. Skin stretched across a sun-dried skeleton could not have looked scrawnier. Deeply shadowed eyes peered brightly, however, from their bony sockets. *Skinniest man I've ever seen, still standin'*, Cole thought.

'Git down an' come in,' the man invited.

'Thanks. Don't mind if I do.'

Cole dismounted, studying the man as he did. Worn clothes hung from his bony shoulders. A large tear in the ragged shirt revealed long underwear beneath. Even through that hole in the shirt it was evident the underwear was as threadbare as the rest of his garments.

The man's trousers, with gaping holes at both knees, ended in ragged threads well above his ankles. Work boots clad both feet, but they, too, had holes in the toes and where bunions bulged the sides. Only the gun and holster strapped high on his hip approached anything of normal standards. Both the gun and its leathers were of good quality and showed careful maintenance.

Cole glanced around. 'Smells like a skunk's been nosin' around after your chickens,' he observed.

The man nodded. 'Skinned one out this mornin',' he explained. 'Hide's worth fifteen cents. I keep a few traps set, 'cause they do keep a-tryin' to find ways into my henhouse at night.'

Cole grinned. 'I'm not sure I'd skin one for fifteen cents.'

The homesteader shrugged. ' 'Tain't so bad after the first whiff or two. Fella's nose sorta gets tired of it, I reckon. Don't notice it much after that. In a couple months, when hides get prime, the price'll go up to pertneart a quarter.'

'I'll take your word for it.' He thrust out a hand that the homesteader took in a bony grip. 'The name's Coleman Black.'

'Jist fixin' to eat a bite,' the man offered without offering his own name in return. ' 'Tain't much, but you're welcome to share a plate.'

Averse to accepting food from a man who

evidently needed it more than he did, Cole contemplated refusing. Even as he did, he knew the refusal would be perceived as a slap in the face. 'I could sure use a bite,' he said instead.

Leaving his horse ground-tied in the bare yard, Cole started for the door. As he did, he spotted the dog. Looking like a cross between a hound and a scarecrow, the long-legged, wiry-haired animal considered him mournfully. He was every bit as scrawny as his master. Cole had the impression he might have at least barked a warning at his approach, but just didn't have the energy.

The inside of the man's cabin was surprisingly clean, but it was as sparsely furnished as the yard. A rough table was flanked by two chairs whose legs and seats had been cobbled and wired together. A bunk of coarse lumber against one wall was covered with a couple ragged blankets and several grain sacks that had been opened out to serve as supplements. The bed had nothing for a pillow.

Beside the door a rifle leaned against the corner. In contrast with the rest of the place, it appeared to be in perfect condition. There was the barest hint of oil coating it, and no trace of rust evident. *At least he takes care of his guns,* Cole approved to himself.

A kitchen range served as both heat and cooking-stove. A cast-iron skillet kept warm on a back corner. A small amount of potatoes and several pieces of meat shared space in it. Without a word the man pulled two battered metal plates from a shelf. He carefully measured half of the food on to each of the plates and set them on the table. They were followed by two cups of steaming coffee from the pot that had set beside the skillet.

From a breadbox he retrieved half a loaf of bread. He sliced off two generous pieces, laying one beside each of the plates. 'Been cold for so early,' Cole offered.

The man nodded. 'Gonna take a lot o' wood this winter,' he fretted. 'Well, sit down and dig in.'

Wordlessly the two took chairs and began to eat. The meat was tasty but Cole couldn't identify it. He had thought, sitting down, that it was a rabbit the man had cooked. With the first bite he knew that not to be the case. Laying aside his misgivings he ate the offered food gratefully. The bread, especially, was surprisingly good. 'You make a fine loaf of bread,' he offered.

'Thankee,' the man responded. 'That's one thing my ma taught me well. She always said, 'You shouldn't have to marry just to have decent bread on the table.'

'Smart lady.'

'She was that. Stayed in Tennessee, I did, till I buried her. Then, the very next day, I headed out here.'

Cole nodded inwardly. That explained the traces of Southern accent in the man's words. 'This is a hard country to homestead, though.'

'It ain't been easy,' the man agreed. 'But my ma always said, "Silas Spivey, when I'm dead and gone you get outa these here hills. Go on out West where there's money to be made." '

'Lots of folks have come into these hills for that.'

Spivey snorted. 'They come here lookin' for gold, that's what they come for. Findin' gold ain't the same as makin' an honest livin', by my way of thinkin'.'

Cole disagreed mildly. 'Some of 'em work awfully hard for what little gold they find.'

'They're welcome to it. I don't want none o' their gold. I get by just fine without it. I got a fair bunch o' chickens, so I can sell eggs in town every week. I got three milk cows, so I got milk to sell. I have to take it to town every day in hot weather, to keep it from spoilin', but it's only a couple hours each way, and it keeps my horse exercised.'

Cole pushed his plate back and concentrated on the still hot coffee. 'Fine meal. I'm obliged.'

'I like it,' Spivey responded. 'It's better meat than lots o' things. Most folks don't know what they're missin', not ever eatin' it.'

In spite of the misgivings that rose suddenly within him, Cole kept his voice steady. 'It was right tasty.'

'One of the things the good Lord give us, and we ought not refuse His gifts,' Spivey went on. 'Like I said, the hide's worth fifteen cents now. More when it's prime. There's plenty o' meat on it for a couple meals. Three meals sometimes, if I can keep myself from eatin' too much at a time. I do try to guard myself against gluttony. That's a sin, you know.'

Cole scarcely heard anything after the connection with the meal and the value of the skunk hide had been made. With a churning feeling in his gut, he asked, 'That was skunk?'

'That it was. Good meat, ain't it?'

With an effort to keep his face impassive, Cole responded, 'It was tasty, for a fact. First time I've ever tried it.'

Mentally he vowed, . . . *and the last.*

'I don't get much company. What brings you out this way?'

'There's been quite a few robberies in the area,' Cole explained. 'I'm here to try to find out who's behind them.'

Spivey eyed him more closely. 'You a lawman?'

Cole shook his head. 'Nope. I have been, but I ain't wearin' a badge now. No, I lost the best friend I ever had, though. I aim to find out who bushwhacked him. It seems like the law hasn't been real interested in finding out who's behind the robberies, so I decided it's most likely up to me.'

'I've heard about a couple of them robberies,' Spivey acknowledged. 'Talk around town, you know. Ain't been another one, has there?'

'As a matter of fact, there has. Yesterday morning. A man was shot from ambush less than five miles from here.'

'That so? Who would thata been?'

'His name was Farnsworth Duckett. He owned a ranch over west a ways.'

'I think I've heard the name in town, though I couldn't be sure,' Spivey offered. 'One o' them rich ranch fellas.'

That seemed to be the extent of his interest in the

slain rancher. He continued the thought Cole's announcement had interrupted. 'I go to town most every day in hot weather, you know. Only need to go a couple times a week from now till spring.'

'You sell your eggs and milk to anyone in particular?'

'The café. They buy all I can bring 'em. The Chuck Box café, that is. The one with the sign out front, that looks like it was made by someone what knows how. I don't sell to them as has a saloon along with it. If folks wanta eat there, they'll have to eat stuff I ain't helped to furnish. The whole town's gettin' worse and worse. Goin' to hell in a hand-basket, that's what it's doin'.'

'Gold-rush towns tend to be that way,' Cole agreed.

Spivey nodded sagely. 'That's a fact. The folks at the Chuck Box are all right though. Good folks, they be. They buy my eggs and milk, as much as I can bring 'em. Cream, too, when I can't get the milk there afore it sours. They can still make butter outa the cream after that. Sometimes they buy the sour milk, too. Emma, she makes what she calls "cottage cheese" outa it, even after it clabbers.'

'I've eaten that a time or two. It's not bad.'

Spivey continued as if Cole hadn't spoken. 'Bacon and ham too, when I butcher a hog. Every time I'm there, they give me a bite to eat, too. That's always mighty nice of 'em. They don't have to do that, you know.'

'You haven't noticed any suspicious folks hanging

around in town, by any chance, have you?'

Spivey eyed him sharply. 'Now what do you figure would make folks look suspicious?'

Cole shrugged. 'I don't know, really. Just a sense you might get. Folks making it a point to listen to other people's conversations, maybe, like they're trying to learn who's carrying a lot of money, something like that.'

Spivey shook his head. 'I wouldn't likely notice if they was. I don't pay that much attention to folks, mostly. I just sell what I brung to town, eat a quick bite, and hightail it back here to get my work done. The less I know about what all goes on in that town the better off I am, I figure.'

'Some that hit it rich are pretty hard not to notice.'

'Now that's a fact. Now I'd think they'd keep it to theirselves, even if they did hit it big.'

'They'd sure be better off if they did.'

'It's like my ma always told me. "Silas Spivey," she always said, "it's up to you to make sure you got enough to fall back on if times get hard, but don't you never go struttin' around like some cock-o'-the-walk, makin' out like you got rich, even if you do some day." '

'Good advice.'

'Smart woman, my ma was. O' course, I don't guess I'll never have to worry none about gettin' too rich an' showin' off like that.'

That was, indeed, the least likely thing Cole could imagine happening.

CHAPTER 9

He smiled as he peered beneath the wide brim of his hat. *Right on time*, he mouthed silently.

He didn't need to say it silently. They were much too far away to hear him, even if he had talked in a normal tone of voice. He just didn't need to say it aloud. He was only talking to himself anyway.

Below him and to his right half a mile, the stagecoach had swung into view as it topped the climb up Elk Ridge Pull. It was a hard pull for the horses, and the driver hauled them to a stop to let them blow and rest a few minutes.

That might have been considered the perfect spot, just there, where they always stopped for a few minutes. He just didn't like that spot. There was timber too close, too many big rocks, too much cover available. He liked it better where he was. And it didn't matter to him if the stage was stopped. He could stop it easy enough.

He watched from that distance as three passengers alit from the coach to stretch their legs. Two of them walked a ways away from the conveyance, putting some brush between themselves and it, in order to relieve themselves.

Must be a woman on board today, he mused silently. The shrug of his shoulders at the awareness was more one of attitude than any visible action.

Fifteen minutes or so later everybody clambered back into the vehicle and the driver slapped the reins across the backs of the team. He could hear, carried faintly on the breeze, the 'Heeyaah' as the driver prodded the team to action.

They responded willingly, and the stage resumed its rocking, bumpy course over the uneven road.

They were nearly abreast of his position when he acted. He was hunkered down in a large outcropping of jagged rocks and boulders. He removed his hat and lay it, upside down, on the ground beside him. He laid the barrel of his rifle across the rock he crouched behind, and looked along its barrel.

When he fired, he jacked a second shell into the chamber and fired again so swiftly the second bullet was already on its way before the sound of the first had followed the projectile to its target. The third shot was just as closely behind the second.

At the first shot the stage coach's shotgun guard grunted in surprise and pain. He looked down at his chest, puzzled that he suddenly couldn't even think well enough to know what had happened.

Just as the sound of that shot reached his ears, the left-wheel horse emitted a sharp grunt and collapsed. Its weight in the harness and its body suddenly blocking the wheel brought the stage to a sudden halt. At the third shot the driver threw both arms high into the air and toppled off the high seat.

Three men boiled out of the now stationary stage. All three had handguns held at the ready. As coolly as if he were picking off a row of tin cans, the hidden gunman fired three times in rapid succession. The three men collapsed so closely to the same time that the third was starting to fall before the first had settled to the ground.

Silence descended on the bloody scene, broken only by the frightened squeals and struggles of the rest of the team of horses. In minutes even they settled down, waiting with the patience of long training for someone to unhitch them.

Still the gunman did not stir or show himself. 'C'mon, little lady,' he muttered, that small smile still hovering around the corners of his mouth. 'We know you're in there, or them fellas wouldn'ta gone off that far to relieve theirselves. We know you might even have a gun, huh? Are you waitin' for me to show myself? Keep waitin', little lady. It ain't gonna happen.'

It was fully ten minutes before a pair of boots, almost hidden by the bottom of a long skirt, appeared in the stagecoach's door. They were followed by a young and very pretty woman. She looked frightened, but resolute. Her eyes cast about quickly, trying to determine the source of the attack. Twice her eyes swept right across his hidden vantage point. The second time she must have caught a glimpse of something that identified his location. She looked straight at him, even though he was sure she couldn't see him.

She lifted both hands into the air in the universal signal of surrender. She looked concerned, but not really frightened. She knew the country she was part of. She knew a woman was normally safe from the myriad things that took men's lives. She knew she could count on being treated with some deference and respect, even by outlaws.

Her hands had just reached above her head, hands open, palms toward the rocks in which the gunman crouched. The rifle barked again. She gasped in sudden pain and surprise, falling back against the side of the stage. She stared at the invisible gunman, her eyes reflecting a total lack of understanding, as she slid slowly down the side of the coach. She ended up sitting on the ground, her shoulders against the step, her hands lying palms up to either side of her, her head tilted back at an awkward angle where it had come to rest against the floor of the stage.

Only then did the gunman stand from his own cover. He stood up, put his hat on, turned his back on the stage and walked back through the rocks.

A hundred yards away, well hidden in a copse of aspen trees, his horse stood waiting placidly. He carefully reloaded his rifle and slid it into the saddle scabbard. He untied the animal from the small tree trunk, fed the off rein up over the horse's neck, stepped into the stirrup and mounted.

He rode directly to the stage at a trot. Once there, he lifted a length of steel bar from where it had hung, tied to one of his saddle strings. Gripping it, he climbed up on top of the stage. He shoved the steel bar through the loop of the padlock that held the strongbox closed. Pulling with all his might, with one foot braced against it, he was rewarded with the ripping sound of the hasp pulling loose from the box.

He climbed back down and replaced the steel bar on his saddle. He took the saddle-bags from behind the cantle, climbed back up on top and emptied the contents of the strongbox into his saddle-bags. Then he climbed down and replaced them on his horse. He carefully went through the pockets of the men and the lady's purse, taking with him every article of value he could find. He led his horse back to the spot where it had been tethered. He cut a low branch from a pine tree and retraced his steps to the stagecoach. Using the branch, he brushed out all tracks of himself and his horse, leaving no marks in the ground that a tracker could use to identify man or mount.

When he was back at his horse he continued in the same way, careful to include both the spot where he had lain in wait, and the place his horse had waited. He brushed away his trail all the way to a wide expanse of bare rock that would leave no trace of his passing. Only then did he drop the branch, mount his horse, and ride off at a swift trot.

He was well out of sight when he heard the first

shout of alarm from some passer-by on the road who had discovered the scene of carnage. He smiled at that, the first real change of expression he had shown throughout.

CHAPTER 10

'I'd make it plumb worth your while.'

Cole looked back into the desperate eyes of the man before him. 'Sorry,' he said. 'I just ain't for hire.'

'Then how am I gonna get the money for my next wagon o' merchandise delivered? Because of all the robbing an' killing going on around here, they won't ship me one blessed thing unless I get the money to 'em ahead of time. How am I supposed to do that?'

Cole raised his eyebrows, but gave no other expression. 'I know it's a tough situation, but I've got my hands full as it is.'

Levi Silverstein, owner of Deadwood's largest mercantile store, glared in response. 'And just what are you so dad-blamed busy with that you can't help out a man in need?'

Cole sighed, trying hard to maintain his patience. 'I'm just as concerned as you are about the situation. That's the whole reason I'm here. One of the people who was murdered was a mighty good friend of mine. I'll find out who's doing it, sooner or later.'

'That don't help me a bit,' the other retorted. 'I need someone to get this cash to North Platte.'

'Why don't you just take it yourself?'

The man snorted derisively. 'Like I'd make it five miles outa town if I tried!'

'So send it with someone you trust that nobody knows has it.'

'I've thought of that. Just like that cattleman did. Who would've even guessed a seasoned rancher would trust a cocky kid like that with his money? I'm tellin' you, whoever's doin' this has ears all over Deadwood. It's plumb eerie. It's like the devil himself is tellin' 'im who has money and when.'

'It sure does seem like it,' Cole agreed.

'Just like that stagecoach,' Silverstein continued. 'He knew that stage carried the payroll for that little mine they're callin "Homestake". He knew the money was on it, he knew when it was gonna get here, and he knew how it'd be guarded.'

'It sure seemed that way,' Cole agreed. 'And they killed everyone before they even showed themselves.'

'What do you mean, "they"? Do you know something the rest of us don't? Is it more than one person?'

Cole shrugged. 'I don't know any more than you do. It does seem like a bit of a stretch to think one man could just lie back and shoot that many people. He'd have to be awfully quick on the trigger and never miss.'

'So you think it's more than one?'

'I don't know.'

'Are you Cole Black?' They were interrupted by a tall man with a drooping moustache. The moustache was noticeably red, but his hair was closer to blond than red. His eyes were as clear and pale blue as Martha McLauren's. A town marshal's badge adorned the front of his vest.

He passed on the opportunity to use his favorite line of humor again. 'I am that. And you'd be Marshal McLauren, I'd guess.'

'Good guess. My daughter told me I'd likely find you here.'

'Wasn't really a guess. She's got your eyes.'

The marshal's voice was dry as he responded, 'You'd oughta know. I understand you've spent some considerable time starin' into them lately.'

'She's a remarkable woman.'

'She is all of that,' the marshal agreed. 'Are you lookin' for a job?'

'Not at the moment. As a matter of fact, I just turned one down. Why?'

'Mind if I sit down?'

Cole waved to a chair. The marshal had no more than gotten seated when the bartender stopped beside the table. 'Coffee, Marshal?'

'Yeah, if it ain't been sittin' on the fire all day, Hemp.'

The bartender grinned. 'If it won't run outa the pot on its own, I'll thin it down some.'

'Fair enough.' He turned his attention back to Cole. 'Hemp makes the best coffee in town, even if he is a barkeep,' he offered. Then he waved a hand at the large mug in front of Cole. 'I see you're already checkin' him out.'

'It'd peel the bark off of a plum bush, but it's good and fresh,' he approved.

The marshal nodded. 'Martha tells me you're here to work on findin' out who's tryin' to thin out the population single-handed.'

Cole nodded. 'One of the guys killed was a close friend of mine.'

'That's what she told me. Any leads?'

'Not a one, so far. How about you?'

The marshal shrugged. 'None that ain't got more holes in 'em than a prairie dog town.'

'So how'm I gonna get that money to North Platte so I can get some supplies in here?' Silverstein interrupted.

Cole appraised the man carefully, a novel idea percolating in the back of his mind. 'Are you desperate enough to try something nobody would ever think of?'

The merchant's eyes grew suddenly guarded. 'What d'ya mean?'

'I mean I think I know someone that could get that money there without a problem, if you'd trust him to do it.'

'Who's that?'

Cole glanced around the half-empty saloon to be sure nobody was surreptitiously listening in on the conversation. He leaned forward across the table, causing the merchant to do the same. 'Have you noticed the swamper here in Number Six?'

'The darky?'

Cole nodded. 'His name's Gideon. Well, he goes by Gideon. His name, believe it or not, is Revelation Sword White. He's a good man. Honest as the day is long, and fair-to-middlin' with a gun. He's probably the last man in Deadwood anyone would think about carryin' a chunk of money like that.'

The merchant snorted. 'Do you think I'd hand that kind of money to a darky and ask him to take it halfway across the country for me? Fat chance I'd have of ever seeing either him or my money again.'

Cole shrugged. 'You could do worse.'

Seth McLauren's eyes darted back and forth from Cole to the merchant. It was obvious he was trying to determine whether Cole was serious or playing some sort of gag on the desperate store-owner. At last the merchant said, 'Would you stand good for the money, if I was to do that?'

'I'd stand good for him,' Cole suggested. 'I wouldn't stand good for it if he ended up gettin' shot like the others have.'

The merchant stared hard at him for several minutes, then stood. 'I'll give it some thought,' he promised as he left.

As soon as he was gone, Cole addressed McLauren. 'What do you know about the Englishman?'

'Miles?'

'Yeah, I think that's his name.'

The marshal stared into space contemplatively for a long moment. 'Well, I can't say I know a thing about him, except he's a dang good poker-player, soft-spoken fella, and as quick and dangerous as a rattlesnake.'

'Why do you say that?'

'He's killed a couple guys here in town. Both times it was pretty clear-cut self-defense. Both of 'em accused him of cheatin' at the cards, but nobody else at the table thought he was. Each of 'em pulled his gun first. And Miles didn't even bat an eye, from what everybody said. His gun just showed up in his hand without anyone seeing him draw. Didn't hesitate. Killed both men outright, then went on about his business as if nothin' happened.'

'Cool, huh?'

'Cool as a cup o' coffee that's been saucered and blowed.'

'I hear he always has a lot of money.'

'He does that. Eats nothin' but the best stuff in town. Drinks the best booze he can find in a boom town, but never drinks too much. Dresses like the Prince of England. Doesn't do a dad-blamed thing to earn any money, except play poker. He wins more than he loses, I 'spect, but not enough to finance his lifestyle.'

'Where does he live?'

'He rents three rooms from Mrs Flanders. She's got a big room-and-board house on the street that runs up the draw just past Number Thirteen. Pays his rent right on time. Keeps his rooms neat as a pin. She thinks he's the best roomer this side o' paradise.'

'What's he doin' in Deadwood?'

'Danged if I know. He's an odd one, but he ain't

done nothin' questionable enough to give me an excuse to quiz 'im too hard.'

'Did you ever check with the bank, to see where his money comes from?'

The marshal's eyebrows lifted. 'Well, now, that's somethin' I hadn't even thought of doin', to be right honest.'

He pulled a watch from his vest pocket and checked it. 'I'll tell you what, the bank's open now. How 'bout you an' me wanderin' down there an' see if the banker's in the mood to spill any information.'

They finished the last dregs of the strong coffee in their mugs and left Number Six together. The teller at the bank showed them to the bank president's office at once.

'Well, good morning, Marshal McLauren,' the banker greeted. 'What brings you into the bastion of financial security this morning?'

'Just wonderin' if you had any of that there security left over for us little fellas,' the marshal rejoined.

'On the salary the town pays you?' the banker responded. 'There's not much security to be had there, I'm afraid.'

'That's what I was afraid of. J.J., this here's Cole Black. He's workin' with me on tryin' to solve this string o' robberies and murders goin' on. Cole, this is J.J. Lewiston. He's a good man, even if he is a banker.'

The banker extended a soft, fleshy hand, but his grip was strong as he shook Cole's hand. 'Happy to meet you,' he said. 'What can I do for you boys this morning?'

'We need some information on Miles Masters.'

The banker's eyes grew cautious instantly. 'What kind of information?'

'Mostly where he gets his money,' the marshal said without preamble. 'He's always got plenty of it, and sure doesn't do any work. He's slicker'n snot on a brass doorknob with that gun of his, and cool as ice usin' it. Does he ever make a big deposit after one of these robberies?'

Lewiston relaxed visibly. He even chuckled slightly. 'No, you don't have to worry about him being involved in any nefarious business. He has no need for money. His family is probably one of the wealthiest families in England.'

'What's he doin' in Deadwood, then?' Cole demanded.

'He just seems to be fascinated with the Wild West in the "New World",' the banker explained. 'He intends to stay in this country for a year or two, then go back to England. "On a lark", he calls it. I've gotten to know him quite well, socially. And, just to put your minds at ease, when the robbery of the stagecoach occurred the other day, he was at my house, so I can assure you with absolute certainty that he was not involved in that matter at all.'

Seth MacLauren and Cole exchanged a look that eloquently expressed their disappointment that what they thought a good lead had fizzled so quickly and decisively.

It didn't occur to either man to even wonder if there was any nefarious connection between the banker and the Englishman.

CHAPTER 11

'Hey, boy! Where'd you get that horse?'

Gideon reined in, unsure how to respond to the pair who blocked his path.

The first thing that passed through his mind, when they stepped out to block his way, was relief. From everything he knew, if the rampant killer had learned he carried such a large amount of cash, he would simply have been shot from ambush. That was the way all the other killings had been done.

The second thing that rushed into his mind was a surge of irritation and anger. He had hoped to never, ever, be called, 'boy,' again. Maybe these were Southerners, using the term of disdain for any member of the black race. Maybe they used it in the general manner in which it was commonly used for almost anyone in the West. Whichever it was, it raised his hackles.

Only trailing along behind those two surges of emotion did tendrils of fear begin to assert their hold on his mind.

'He's my horse,' Gideon responded, forcing himself to omit the 'suh,' that he habitually wanted to add.

'That ain't what I asked,' the man insisted. 'I asked where you got him.'

Gideon lifted his chin slightly. His voice was suddenly defiant. 'I got him from the man what owned him afore I did, just the same as I reckon you got yours.'

The two men exchanged looks of surprise and sudden caution. Both held rifles, almost casually pointed at Gideon. Both also wore Colt .45s, well-worn, tied down. One of them nodded his chin at Gideon's pistol. 'He's wearin' a fine lookin' hogleg hisself,' he pointed out to his companion.

The other man stepped over where he could see it. 'He is at that. Can you use that thing,' boy?'

Gideon declined to answer, weighing his chances, considering leaning forward, low on the horse's neck and spurring him to sudden flight. Even as he considered it, he knew it would only result in his being shot in the back.

'I said, can you use that gun, boy?' The man's voice was raised several decibels, insistent and demanding.

His companion grinned. 'I bet he can't, Len. I bet he'd take pertneart three heartbeats to haul it outa the holster, and three more to stop shakin' enough to squeeze the trigger.'

The other eyed Gideon speculatively. 'You think so? Maybe we'd oughta find out. That's a fine horse, anyway. We could use another horse, once he ain't got no use for it.'

'Want me to knock 'im off of it?'

'Naw. Let's see if he can use that thing.'

'What're you thinkin', Len?'

Instead of answering, he addressed Gideon. 'Get down off that horse, boy. I'm gonna give you a white man's chance to show me whether you can use that thing.'

When Gideon failed to move, he lifted his rifle barrel more threateningly. 'I said, get down off that horse.'

Faced with no choice, Gideon stepped from the saddle. As he did, his hand brushed the butt of his .45, making sure the thong that held it in its holster was unfastened.

'I'll tell you what I'm gonna do, boy,' the rifleman named Len said. 'I'm gonna lay down my rifle. Then I'll give you a chance to see if you can outdraw me. Dave here will fire his rifle up in the air. That'll be the signal to go for your gun. If you're real fast, you just might beat me to the draw. Of course, there ain't nobody done that yet, but you might. At least I'll give you a fightin' chance.'

'I don't think you even need to hurry none, Len,' the one named Dave responded with a malicious grin. 'He looks to me like he's so scared he's about to wet his pants. He ain't gonna be none too fast.'

Len grinned in response. He lowered the hammer on his rifle and laid it on the ground. He spread his legs slightly and dropped his hand to hover just above his gun butt. 'Any time you're ready, Dave. Let 'er rip.'

Gideon might have offered a verbal response if the hard knot in his throat hadn't made even breathing a challenge. He had listened well to all of Cole's instructions. He had practiced diligently, every day. He had practiced without ammunition in his room. He had practiced with ammunition on the occasions when he could get away from town to do so. He had taken to heart Cole's demand that he practice drawing and shooting fifty times every day.

At first, his hand and arm ached with the unaccustomed effort, rendering it impossible to continue that many times. Once past the first soreness, however, it became increasingly easy to do so. He found that he was far quicker than he had ever imagined he could be. He was also uncannily accurate when he was able to use ammunition and combine the repetitions with firing at a target.

That was vastly different from drawing against another human being, knowing only one of them would survive. It was compounded by his opponent having a friend at his side armed with a rifle. Even so, he was, once again, in a dilemma from which there was no escape. Just as when he had sat with a noose around his neck, he looked death in the face and chose not to flinch. If he were to die this day, he would do so as a man. A free man.

He brushed his hand along the familiar butt of his forty-five, waiting for the signal.

Without giving any visual indication he was about

to do so, Dave fired his rifle into the air.

It was much quicker than Gideon had anticipated. It was also much louder. Instead of flinching away from the noise, however, his startled reaction was to instantly close his hand on the butt of his gun and carry through with the motion he had rehearsed countless times.

Fast enough for it to be only a blur to the watching rifleman, his gun swept up from its holster, belching fire and lead at the exact instant it leveled toward the gunman who had forced his hand. The bullet slammed into the center of his chest when his own gun was only halfway out of its holster. He staggered backward a step, a short gasping cough escaping through his lips. He continued the draw of his gun, but his hand contracted spasmodically, firing it into the ground before it fell from his suddenly lax hand. His eyes betrayed total confusion. That he might have been beaten by this ragged-looking black man had never entered his mind as a possibility. He was dead before he was able to process what had happened.

Dave stared in open-mouthed surprise for just an instant. Then he swore and whipped his rifle toward Gideon, squeezing the trigger as he did.

Nothing happened. His stunned surprise at seeing his friend outdrawn caused him to forget to lever another shell into the rifle's chamber. He did not have the opportunity to do so.

As if he had done so a dozen times before, Gideon swung his .45 to the second man and dispatched him with a single bullet to the chest.

He stood there, a thin tendril of smoke rising from his gun barrel, trying to process the events that had just taken place. Then he began to shake. Sweat broke out on his forehead. With a trembling hand he replaced the Colt in its holster. He swallowed hard twice, then bent forward and lost the contents of his stomach on to the road.

When his retching passed, he suddenly remembered one of Cole's sterner lectures. He drew his pistol, ejected the two spent cartridges, and replaced them with fresh. Then he replaced it, fastening the thong that would keep it from falling from the holster.

He studied the two dead men lying in the road. His mission was urgent. He could not take time to bury the pair.

They must have been camped close by, watching the road for prospective victims to rob. Glancing around, he caught a thin wisp of smoke from within a small clump of trees a dozen yards from the road. He considered checking out their campsite, then reconsidered at once. They had nothing he wanted or needed. The more distance he put between himself and this place the better.

He stepped into the saddle, guided his horse carefully around the two dead men, then nudged him to a swift trot. Even so, every few yards he turned his head and looked back until the road turned and there was no longer anything to see behind him.

CHAPTER 12

Coleman Black and Martha McLauren watched the exchange with equal measures of mixed emotions.

They sat together, eating lunch in the Chuck Box café. At a table a short distance away, Silas Spivey was served a meagre plate of biscuits and gravy.

They had observed the ritual before. Cole had shared with Martha the story of eating at the homesteader's. It had become a point of ongoing humor between them. Twice she had invited Cole to eat with her and her father. Each time he had jokingly quizzed her carefully to make sure she wasn't also feeding him skunk meat.

He had also shared the homesteader's gratitude that the café usually fed him when he brought in eggs and milk. On more than one occasion they had observed him carefully wiping the last traces of gravy from the plate with the last piece of biscuit, wasting nothing. They shared an equal skepticism of the owners' generosity, noting that the meal they always provided for Spivey was the cheapest thing they could offer. Biscuits and meatless gravy would scarcely keep a man going.

Another patron of the café obviously thought so as well. Miles Masters approached Spivey. 'I say, my good man, might I join you?'

Spivey looked up in obvious surprise. Normally he spoke to nobody, nor was he usually spoken to. After a moment's hesitation, he said, 'Fine with me.'

Miles laid his expensive bowler carefully on a corner of the table and took the chair across from Spivey. 'It is far too fine a day for one to dine alone, wouldn't you say?'

Spivey eyed him warily without raising his head from where it was poised above his plate of thin gravy over a single, halved biscuit. 'Right sunny for a fact,' he agreed.

It would have been impossible to imagine a more marked contrast between two individuals. On one side of the table, an impeccably dressed, carefully groomed gentleman, emitting faint traces of very expensive perfume, radiated health and well-being. On the other side of the table a totally unkempt, unshaven ragamuffin, looking more akin to a scarecrow than a living person, emitted a far more earthy odor of sweat and poverty.

Just then the waitress approached. 'Lunch, Mr Masters?'

Masters pursed his lips thoughtfully. 'Yes indeed, but I think not the usual today, my dear,' he replied.

He addressed the scrawny homesteader across the table. 'I say, my good man, I have had an unusually good run of luck at the gaming table, and I should like to celebrate. If you would care to join me in doing so, I should like to dine on the finest steak this establishment offers, with the best of accoutrements as well. May I be honored by your allowing me to replace that biscuit and gravy with one of the same?'

As he spoke, the words slowly sank into Spivey's consciousness that the Englishman was offering to buy him a meal. The best meal in the house, no less. His jaw clamped increasingly tight as Miles spoke. By the end of Miles's request, the muscles bulged at the hinges of his jaw. His face increasingly reddened. As Miles completed the offer, Spivey stood abruptly. The chair flew backward, crashing to the floor. Spivey pointed a bony finger, shaking with its fury, at the Englishman.

It took three starts before the apoplectic homesteader could make words issue from his mouth. As he tried, he kept jabbing the quivering, bony finger at Miles. When at last he finally found his voice, he sputtered, 'Why, you uppity, highfalutin, fancy talkin' cock-o'-the-walk dandy, I ain't got no need o' charity from the likes o' you nor nobody else. Silas Spivey stands on his own two feet an' ain't never took no charity from nobody. And if 'n I was starvin' plumb to death I'd not take a crumb from the likes o' you, what spends no time makin' an honest livin', just hangin' around them pits of iniquity with their booze and whores and gamblin'. What's more, it'll be a cold day in perdition when I ever even sit down at a table with the likes o' you agin!'

With that he stalked toward the door. Halfway there he stopped in his tracks. He whirled back, stomped to the table and grabbed the plate with its biscuit and gravy, picked up his fork, and strode to the door, head jutted forward, eyes glaring wildly.

Outside the door he walked several paces and sat down on the edge of the board sidewalk. There he ate the meager meal, once again wiping the plate clean of every last trace of gravy. When he had finished, he walked back into the café, sat the plate and fork on the nearest empty table to the door, whirled back outside, and marched angrily down the street.

Miles Masters sat there the whole time, staring in silent disbelief. Only when Spivey had passed out of sight down the street did he move. Then he addressed Cole and Martha. 'I say! I'm afraid I insulted the chap.'

Cole nodded, swallowing a bite of food before he replied. 'He's a poor man, but he's got a lot of pride.'

'But, but,' the Englishman protested, 'even bully beef would be a veritable feast compared to what the poor man lives on. And I offered no charity. At least I tried very hard to extend an invitation to join me in celebration, rather than an act of charity, by which he might be put off.'

'I guess you didn't disguise it well enough,' Martha offered. 'He evidently still thought it sounded like charity.'

Whether by the rebuff of his offer, or the castigation of his morals and lack of work ethic, it was

Miles's turn to become angry. Staring after the disappeared homesteader, his visage became increasingly clouded. After a few minutes of glaring silence, he stood, placed his bowler carefully on his head, and stalked out the door.

Martha actually giggled, watching him leave. 'At least Mr Spivey remembered he hadn't eaten yet.'

Cole grinned. 'It was a free meal.'

'It surprised me that he didn't accept the steak,' Martha said.

Cole shook his head. 'I'm not sure he'd accept anything offered as a gift.'

Martha disagreed at once. 'He will sometimes. Do you know Rowdy Hansen?'

Cole frowned. 'The name rings a vague bell. I think I've heard it. I don't know him.'

'He's a cowboy who works for different ranches around. Miles hired him for a hunting guide last fall.'

'Hunting guide?'

She nodded. 'He wanted to, how did he put it, "experience the fabled thrill of large-game hunting in the American West." He hired Rowdy to take him up in the hills deer hunting. Rowdy told me he shot a really nice buck, but didn't know what to do with it after he got it. He had Rowdy take it by Mr Spivey's homestead, tell him about the hunt, and offer him the deer. He told Mr Spivey that all that good meat would just go to waste otherwise, and he took it.'

'It's getting to where there isn't a lot of wild game around here to waste,' Cole observed.

Martha's mood darkened instantly in response. 'That's true. All these people flocking into this country looking for gold have just about shot everything that moves in the hills, just to survive until they make that big strike they're never going to make.'

Cole started to answer, but was interrupted by shouts from the street. As if by the same volition, the two stood from the table and headed for the door.

A crowd was already beginning to gather at the far end of Deadwood's main (and nearly only) street. A train of three heavily loaded freight wagons lumbered along, bringing badly needed supplies. At the head of the wagons, riding beside the wagon master, rode Gideon, looking for all the world like a triumphant legionnaire, riding in a victory parade.

'He made it!' Martha cried.

Levi Silverstein rushed up beside them, wiping his hands in the large apron he always wore. 'Well, well!' he exulted. 'Well, well! Four wagons! Four! And he must have bartered well. He actually did it!'

'I told you he could be trusted,' Cole reminded the merchant.

'Well, well! Well, well! Well, I guess you did. I guess you were right. I honestly thought I'd thrown a couple thousand dollars away, I have to admit. Well, well! I'm back in business!'

'That's no small accomplishment, getting through with the money and getting those four wagons back here.'

'No, indeed,' the store owner agreed. 'No, indeed.

Well, well. Fine thing.'

'I hope you remember that when you pay the man,' Cole admonished.

The merchant looked at him sharply. 'You think I would cheat the man? Mr Black, my people know as well as his what it is like to be scorned, cheated, robbed and reviled. Though much less deserving of that scorn in our case, I would say. Nevertheless, I will most certainly pay him every penny I promised him.'

Martha's voice had an almost acrid edge as she said, 'I suspect you can afford to, since you'll be able to name your price for almost everything he's brought you,' she said.

Just then Gideon galloped over to where he had spotted Cole. 'I done it, Cole! I made it through all the way to North Platte, an' I done brung back ever'thin' Mistah Silverstein asked for.'

'Did you have any trouble?'

The jubilance left Gideon's face, replaced by a look of foreboding. 'Well, suh . . . I mean, Cole . . . I did have a bit of a problem less'n ten miles out.'

'The pair out by Baldwin's Knob?'

'Yessuh. That be the ones. They was fixin' to kill me an' take my horse an' things. I just couldn't let that happen, Mistah . . . uh, Cole. I just couldn't let Mr Silverstein down, when he'd done trusted me like nobody had ever trusted me in all my born days.'

'What happened?'

'Well, they made me get down off my horse. They both had rifles a-pointed right at me. Then one of 'em decided it'd be fun to make me draw agin 'im, so

94

he laid down 'is rifle an' tol' the other fella to shoot in the air. When he shot, we was both s'posed to draw. He was plumb sure he could kill me easy, me just bein' a ragged darky an' all. But I done been practicin' all the time, jus' like you tol' me to, Cole. I done been practicin' till I's plumb fast. I done beat 'im to the draw an' shot im plumb dead center.'

'Good for you,' Cole approved.

Gideon continued. 'Then the other fella, he tried to shoot me with his rifle, only he forgot he'd done shot the shell in the barrel already. Afore he could get another shell into it, I done had to shoot him too.'

Martha looked back and forth from Gideon to Cole as the narrative unfolded. 'That's almost exactly what Father had figured out,' she concurred. 'Except he thought the one with the rifle had missed, somehow, since he'd fired one shot. Someone found them dead in the road and reported it to Father. He said it looked exactly like they had tried to rob someone on the road. And whoever killed them hadn't even ridden over to their campsite to steal anything.'

'They didn't have nothin' I wanted,' Gideon protested. 'They was tryin' to rob me. I wasn't mindin' to rob them. Does you reckon I's in trouble on account of I had to kill them fellas?'

Cole shook his head. 'I wouldn't think so. It was clearly self-defense, even from what the marshal was able to make out.'

Martha spoke up again. 'There was a five-hundred-dollar reward on one of them, though.'

Gideon's eyes lit up instantly. 'They was?'

Martha nodded. 'We have a flyer from down in Kansas on one of them. All we have to do is send them proof of his death, and they'll telegraph the money to the bank here for you.'

'Well, now, whatd'ya know!' Gideon exulted. 'Five hundred dollars!'

He might have said more, but Silverstein was urgently waving him toward his mercantile store to help with off-loading the wagons of merchandise, which people were already lining up to buy.

CHAPTER 13

Some people are not built to contain any level of excitement. That's true even if the failure to do so is pure foolishness. Sometimes it can put them in dire peril.

Cole and Martha were just finishing lunch at the Chuck Box café when the prospector entered. He carried a pair of saddle-bags. which he kept close at hand.

The waitress approached. 'Hey, Frank, what's in the saddle-bags?'

Openly, the prospector announced, 'Gold. The gold I came out here looking for. Now I can go home.'

All eyes in the café swivelled to focus on the speaker. 'You found gold?' the waitress echoed.

He nodded enthusiastically. 'Found just exactly what I was lookin' for! Nothin' great big. Just a vein that was right along the surface. Just enough to make it worth the chance I took leavin' everything to come all the way out here to have a look.'

'How much did you get, Frank?' another patron shouted across the room.

Frank shrugged. 'Ain't had it weighed or nothin'. Just packed it up to head back East. I 'spect it's three or four thousand dollars' worth, at least.'

'That wouldn't be enough for most guys,' another offered.

'It's plenty for me.' The grimy prospector was positively giddy about his good fortune.

'There's a lot more of it in them hills,' a patron at a different table assured him.

The prospector shook his head. 'There most likely is, all right enough. Others is welcome to it. I left a wife an' two kids back in Iowa to come out here and find gold. I found it. I hacked away at the vein till it was petered out. I got a-plenty to set me and the missus up with a fine farm, where we can raise a family and live decent.'

'Not many are satisfied with that,' Cole observed.

'I think it's wonderful,' Martha countered.

Very quietly, so that none but Martha could hear, Cole said, 'I think it's insanely stupid. With the murders that have been committed around here, to announce publicly you're carrying that kind of gold is worse than stupid.'

Martha's eyes, which moments before had glistened with excitement for the man's good fortune, clouded at once. 'Oh dear! You're right! He's just begging to be another victim. You have to do something!'

Cole's mind was already spinning. He and Martha

made a hasty departure from the café. He escorted her to the marshal's office, then went in search of Gideon. He found him openly flirting with a young woman who worked as a maid for one of the affluent saloon-owners. 'I need to talk with you,' he announced.

Gideon frowned with an unaccustomed show of independence. 'I's sort of busy just now, Cole,' he answered, with none of his former hesitation at using Cole's name.

Cole's voice was harder, more brusque than Gideon had heard it. 'It's urgent,' he said.

Gideon opened his mouth as if to protest again. He looked longingly at the young woman. She returned the look with a coquettish tilt of her head, but said nothing.

He looked back at Cole, and saw there the hard, set lines that telegraphed his friend's urgency. He turned back to the woman. 'I'll be back afore you know it, Lily Mae.'

'Don't be long,' she replied, her voice and posture brimming with invitation. 'The Millers ain't never home in the afternoons.'

Cole thought he heard Gideon groan aloud as he tore himself away and followed him outside. 'What's so plumb awful important?' he complained as soon as they were outside.

'I need your help,' Cole announced. 'A prospector's over at the café announcing to the world that he's heading back to Iowa with two saddle-bags filled with gold.'

Gideon's mouth dropped open. 'Now that there's dumber'n shovin' a bloody hand in a pond full o' alligators!'

Rather than discuss the issue, Cole said, 'Get your guns and your horse and meet me in front of Number Six. We'll trail along a ways behind him, and see if we can keep him from getting killed.'

Gideon cast one quick, longing glance back to the door through which he had just come, then set out on a swift walk to comply.

By the time both men had retrieved their horses and gear, the prospector had a long head-start on them. Spurring their horses, they galloped along the road that led east by southeast, on a path that would take them out of the Black Hills within thirty or forty miles.

The day was clear, but the air was sharp with the promise of winter's rapid approach. Their breath made white vapors in front of their faces, which were instantly snatched away by the wind of their rapid pace.

They were less than two miles out of town when the cold air bore the sound of a single, distant rifle shot. Cole swore and spurred his horse again, leaning over the saddle horn to lessen the drag his body caused. The horse responded, lifting from his easy gallop to an all-out run.

A quarter of a mile later, topping a steep grade, they spotted the hapless prospector's riderless horse, standing in the road.

Beside the horse a dark lump lay on the ground.

Both men knew instantly what it was, and that they were too late.

Eyeing the terrain in front of the fallen victim, Cole yelled, 'Check him to see if he's still alive.'

He guessed at the spot from which the shot should have come, and spurred his horse toward it, hugging the animal's neck to make himself as small a target as possible. His guess proved right, but it might just as well have been wrong. The familiar signs were there that someone had waited in the edge of a fringe of timber. From there he had shot the prospector from the saddle.

The tracks, however, led out of the timber, directly to the victim, then off across a broad stretch of gravelly ground that bore only the faintest traces of a horse's passage.

He returned to where Gideon waited with the fallen prospector. Gideon sat on the ground, tears staining his face. 'We's too late, Cole. We's allays too late. If'n I'd hustled a bunch more, we might've made it quick enough to save 'im, but I was too hunged up, a-thinkin' on Lily Mae, to even think about a fella might die on account o' we was too slow.'

'It's not your fault.' Cole attempted to console his friend. 'It's his own fault, bragging around town about his strike, announcing the direction he was going to go, even. If we'd been quicker, we'd have probably been killed along with him.'

Even as he said it, he silently berated himself with the same lament as was pouring out of Gideon.

Together they hoisted the dead man across his saddle, tied him in place, and began the slow plod back to town.

By the time they arrived, the regret and chagrin roiling within him had been replaced with a hard, cold determination to bring the culprit to justice. Preferably it would be justice at the end of his own gun.

CHAPTER 14

'I say it would be the best possible approach to set a trap for this chap,' Miles argued.

Cole shook his head. 'You'd be putting yourself in a great deal of danger, with no assurance at all that I could keep him from killing you.'

'Nonsense!' the Englishman argued. 'If there are two, or perhaps three of us, with only me being the visible and inviting target, I have perfect confidence you will be able to forestall any dire and untoward consequences.'

'It's too risky.'

'I admit there is an element of risk involved. Perhaps it is exactly that element of risk that makes the whole idea appeal to me. I honestly don't know why I hadn't thought of it much sooner.'

'Putting yourself at risk ain't exactly fun and games.'

'But it does get the heart to pumping,' Miles differed. 'And it is that element of excitement that gives life its zest.'

'I ain't never been that desperate for excitement,' Cole declared. 'And I sure ain't gonna agree to somethin' that puts your life in jeopardy, just to liven up your life.'

'Ah, but I absolutely insist,' Masters countered. 'If you refuse to co-operate, then I will be forced to carry out the ploy entirely on my own.'

'That'd be plumb suicide.'

'Exactly! So your co-operation will serve only to prevent that regrettable event, and you will be in no way responsible for any untoward outcome.'

'Any what?'

'Untoward outcome. You will be in no way responsible if the ploy results in my demise. But if it is successful, we will have joined forces to eliminate a most vexatious nuisance.'

'Why are you so all-fired anxious to get involved?'

For the first time Cole could remember, the Englishman seemed at a loss for words. After a long, thoughtful pause, he said, 'I came here to observe for myself the flavor of frontier life in the American West that we have heard so much about, across the water. After spending some little time here, I determined it was frightfully hollow merely to observe, and I began to involve myself in more and more of the more dashing aspects of life in the West. It has been a most exhilarating experience. Yet, even so, something seems to be persistently absent. After much thought and consideration, I have determined that in all of it, my own well-being was never in any actual jeopardy.'

'When you pulled a gun against guys accusin' you of cheatin' at cards, I'd say your well-being was very much at stake.'

Miles shrugged off the assertion. 'It was unlikely that either of the two louts who threatened me were any match for my skill or marksmanship.'

'Some of 'em can surprise you.'

Miles shrugged again. 'Perhaps, but unlikely. No, I think, in reality, the greatest thing I stood to lose was some amount of money. Having no paucity of that, even such a loss has no great level of threat to me. Now, having carefully considered the matter, I have determined that involving myself in the apprehension of this most nefarious brigand will provide that missing element in my own experience, as well as rendering a valuable service to the country that has been so warmly hospitable to me.'

Cole continued to argue with the determined Englishman for nearly an hour, before acquiescing to the plan.

Though he had reluctantly agreed, Cole's stomach was tied in knots. 'This here's just plumb crazy dumb!' was Gideon's assessment.

'I can't argue with that for a minute,' Cole agreed. 'That's why I need your help. If you ride one wing and I ride the other, and we stay about a hundred yards ahead of him, as much out of sight as we can, we might have a chance to spot the killer before Masters gets himself killed.'

'If we's close enough to spot this fella afore he's done shot Mistah Masters, we's gonna be close enough that he'll spot us. Then he's either gonna hunker down an' let us ride by, or he's gonna shoot us too.'

Cole was hard pressed to offer any rational disagreement. 'That's the problem,' he conceded. 'But he's dead set on doin' it, and I don't know any other way we'll even have a chance. If we stay far enough to either side of the road, there's a chance he'll be watching the road itself and won't spot us.'

Gideon argued far more than was his wont, but eventually agreed to his part in the effort.

Accordingly, Masters was far more vocal than usual that night in talking about how much he had won at the gambling tables. He pretended to have a couple drinks too many, to be far more loquacious than normal, and shared his 'plan' with those close to him. He did so in slightly slurred speech that was clearly audible to any listening ears.

'I am most certainly not so foolish as to keep this amount of money upon my person any longer than necessary,' he assured those around him at the bar. 'I will ride to the budding metropolis of Spearfish at first light, where my winnings will be safely ensconced in my personal account at the bank there.'

Both Cole and Gideon had taken unobtrusive positions in the saloon, watching carefully for anyone who seemed more than normally interested in the Englishman's plan. Even so, they caught no hint of that interest from the shadowed figure who listened most intently.

At first light, Masters set out as announced. Far enough to either side of the road to be unable to even see each other, Cole and Gideon rode a hundred yards ahead of him, watching every pile of rocks, every cluster of trees, every likely-looking patch of brush, for any sign of potential trouble.

It probably wasn't a very good plan to begin with. In a perfect world, it might have worked, even so. It was not a perfect world.

They were scarcely three miles from town when the killer struck. Master's horse stumbled just slightly. He leaned forward just a little to offer the animal a reassuring pat on the neck as his eyes continued to sweep the area before and to either side of him.

Just as he leaned forward, the very expensive bowler hat that he characteristically wore flew from his head. He flung both hands into the air and toppled backward off his horse. He lay unmoving on the ground, a pool of blood instantly staining the dirt beneath his head.

From the corner of his eye Cole saw the hat fly, followed by the Englishman's tumble from the saddle. In the following instant the sound of a single rifle shot slapped against him. He instinctively pinpointed the source of the shot as a clump of aspen trees seventy-five yards ahead of Masters, almost exactly even with his own position.

He instantly leaned forward over the saddle horn and spurred his horse, running directly toward the spot from which the shot had come. The gunman evidently spotted him at once. A small notch magically appeared in the tip of his horse's ear. The animal shook his head once, but maintained his course and speed with stoic obedience. Cole hadn't even time enough to digest the meaning of that sudden split in the tip of his horse's ear when sound of the second shot reached him.

The sound of crashing brush followed at once, as the gunman abandoned the game and took flight.

Without slowing, Cole rode straight into the trees. It was his second miscalculation of the day. He was three horse's lengths into the trees when a low branch swept him from the saddle, sending him crashing to the ground. He lay where he fell for several seconds, fighting to force air back into his lungs with little success. His horse ran a few steps farther, then slowed and stopped. He shook his head again at the unaccustomed stinging of his ear, then stood placidly waiting for his master.

The sounds of the gunman's flight faded into the distance as Cole struggled to get his wind back.

When he had succeeded in sucking in a couple breaths, he rose warily to his feet.

'Cole! Is you OK?'

Gideon's frightened voice called out as he approached in full gallop. 'Here, Gideon,' he called in reply.

'Is you OK?' Gideon repeated.

'Yeah, I'm fine. Just got knocked out of the saddle tryin' to run my horse through the timber.'

'Did you get him?'

'No. I didn't even see him. He took a shot at me, too, but missed. Then he took off. I was trying to follow him by sound, and my horse went under a branch too low for me to duck.'

'He's plumb awful quick, he is.'

'He got Masters.'

'Yessuh, but not that bad, I's thinkin'.'

'What? He's alive?'

'Yessuh. He's breathin' all right enough. He's out cold, but he's breathin'. He's got a furrow along the top of his head like'n a plow done made it, but he's alive.'

Cole looked back and forth from Gideon to the timber in the direction the gunman fled. After a minute's thought, he said, 'Why don't you see what you can do for him. I'll see if I can find some tracks.'

Without a word, Gideon turned his horse and trotted back to tend to the downed Englishman. Moving much more slowly and carefully, Cole followed the trail of broken branches and smashed brush left behind in the gunman's wake.

There was nothing distinguishable except for the broken vegetation until the man had mounted his horse and ridden away at a dead run. Even there, the tracks were few and faint. Even with the threat of pursuit hounding him, the gunman had taken the pains to steer his horse away from any soft ground, zigzagging as necessary to stay on rocky terrain.

Anger boiled within Cole. He had been so close, and he was as empty-handed as ever, with no more to go on than he had started out the day with.

He turned back, dismounted and followed the horse's tracks back to where it had been tethered in wait, studying the path it had taken more carefully. He had nearly given up finding anything of value, when one hoofprint caught his eye.

In a spot of softer ground near the base of a large tree, he spotted one clear hoofprint. He bent over, studying it closely. 'Well, look at that! His horse has one busted shoe,' he muttered. 'It ain't splayed out sideways or anything, though. Wonder what's keepin' the busted piece in place.'

Beyond that, he was able to find nothing of value, in spite of the haste of the gunman's flight.

By the time he got back to Gideon and Masters, Miles was sitting up, holding a bloody silk kerchief on top of his head. 'Are you OK?' Cole asked as he approached.

'Quite alive at least,' Masters responded. 'Of that I'm quite certain. My head would not hurt nearly this much if I weren't. I say, this is even worse than a hangover!'

Cole dismounted and picked up the bowler. He stuck his finger through the bullet hole in the front of it, and another finger through the hole in the other side. 'That's the first time this guy's missed, as far as I can tell,' he observed.

'I say, he didn't entirely miss, as I am fully aware at the moment,' Miles argued.

'I'd say he missed quite a ways,' Cole disagreed. 'He's never shot anyone in the head before. He's shot every one I know of right in the heart. I wonder why he went for a head shot.'

'I leaned forward just then,' Miles said, realizing as he said it that he owed his life to his horse's stumble. 'My horse stumbled, and I leaned forward to stroke his neck in reassurance. Oooh, my head hurts.'

'Do you think you can make it back to town?'

Masters looked up at his saddle. He began to gather himself. 'I say, if you chaps will help me into the saddle, I shall give it my most valiant effort.'

CHAPTER 15

'Gideon still thinks it's Masters.'

Martha stared at Cole as if suspecting him of some sort of trick. 'How could he possibly think that?'

Cole simply shrugged his shoulders. 'I told him we'd talked to the banker. He said that maybe the banker's in it together with him. He doesn't trust bankers very much.' He went back to giving his full attention to the cup of coffee he cradled in both hands.

Marshal MacLauren picked up the thread of conversation. 'How does he explain Masters gettin' shot?'

'He thinks it was a set-up, just to divert suspicion. He thinks Masters hired someone to shoot his hat off, makin' it look like he was tryin' to kill him. He thinks it was an accident that he shot too low and split his scalp open.'

'Do you think so?' Martha demanded.

Cole shook his head. 'Not really. It's a possibility, I suppose, but Masters has a good enough alibi for every time the killer's struck to make it unnecessary to go to that extreme. No, I don't think so. I think he's an idiot, making himself a target like that, but I don't think he's the killer.'

The marshal chuckled unexpectedly. 'I bet he'll decide he was an idiot too, by the time his head quits hurtin'.'

'He's got a pretty deep gouge across the top of it,' Cole agreed. 'Gideon said if he didn't keep himself so clean, he could plant potatoes in that furrow. He lost a lot of blood out there. I was sure he was a dead man when I saw him lyin' there in that puddle of blood.'

Martha agreed. 'I saw him in the café yesterday. He's still as white as a sheet. He stood up too fast when he was through eating, and nearly passed out, it looked like.'

'He hasn't replaced his hat, I noticed.'

The marshal agreed. 'He's as proud as a peacock of that hat. I'm guessin' he'll wear it clear back to England when he goes. He's sure got his souvenir of the "Great American West".'

'And a scar clear across the top of his head to go along with it,' Martha added.

'So what are you going to do next, Cole? Any ideas?' the marshal demanded.

Cole finished his cup of coffee before he answered. As he set it back on the table he said, 'To be real honest, I don't know, Seth. I think I'll ride back out there and look the area over a lot better. I was in kind of a hurry, so there might be something in the tracks he left, if I look close enough.'

'You didn't see anything much, though, huh?'

Cole hesitated, wondering whether to divulge what he had seen. He decided if he couldn't trust Martha and her father, he couldn't trust anyone. 'Actually, I did see one thing that I think might end up being helpful.'

Both Martha and her father stared at him, waiting in silence for him to continue. 'I have to look closer, but it looked at first glance like his horse has one busted shoe.'

'A broken horseshoe?' Martha echoed.

Cole nodded. 'Like I said, I was in a hurry. I didn't know how bad Miles was hit. Then Gideon and I felt like we had to get him back to town before we did anything else. But yeah, it sure looked like it was broken.'

'Well, that'd be somethin' we could maybe follow up on,' Seth opined. 'I can check with the blacksmith, to see if someone's come in to get a busted shoe replaced. What hoof?'

'Right front.'

'That'd sure be somethin' a man'd be likely to notice. His horse shoulda been limpin'.'

Cole nodded. 'You'd think so, anyway. Like I said, I want to take a closer look.'

Martha laid a hand on his arm. The warmth of her hand radiated up his arm, filling every part of his being with a sudden flush of pleasure. That surge of pleasure tripled as she said, 'Oh, Cole, be careful! I don't know what I'd do if something happened to you.'

Her sudden show of emotion caught Cole by surprise. He had been struggling for days with his own emotions, not knowing if she felt the same about him. The look in her eyes now left no doubt of that.

'Gettin' awful mushy in here for me,' the marshal said, standing and picking up his hat. 'I'm headin' back to the office.'

He walked out his front door, leaving Martha and Cole alone, staring into each other's eyes. He wasn't past his front walk when they were in each other's arms instead.

CHAPTER 16

Walking, leading his horse, Cole followed the faint trail left by the fleeing gunman. It was the hardest thing he could remember doing, leaving Martha at home, riding out here to pursue the purpose for which he had ridden to Deadwood.

He had always concentrated, almost compulsively, on whatever task lay before him. The single-minded obsession with which he did so left no room for any conflicting distractions. Now, suddenly, he found himself constantly thinking about Martha, instead of what he was doing. He woke several times a night, dreaming about her. For the past several weeks he had found every excuse imaginable to spend time with her. Now he knew she felt as strongly about him as he did about her. Joy surged continually within him until he thought he would burst if he didn't shout his love to the four winds.

Even so, he couldn't consider pursuing anything with her until he had solved the crimes he had come here to deal with. He owed that to Danny. He owed that to Harrington. He owed that to himself.

He realized with a start that he had covered the last half a mile on foot with his mind several miles away from what he was supposed to be doing. He cursed silently, forcing his attention back fully on the trail he had managed to continue tracing, even while thinking of everything else instead.

After the first mile, the gunman had ceased to be as careful to keep to hard and rocky ground. More and more of his tracks were clearly visible. As they crossed a shallow arroyo, in the moist dirt along the bottom, he found what he had long sought. Several clear, sharp hoofprints were impressed in the soft earth. They were so clear and sharp he could make out the heads of the nails holding the horse's shoes in place.

At one print in particular, he squatted and studied a long while.

'Ain't never seen that done,' he mused. 'His horse busted a shoe. That ain't unusual. What's unusual is that the fella obviously knows it, but didn't fix it. He put an extra nail in the busted piece, to keep it on the horse, so he didn't have to go to town and have the blacksmith shoe it.'

He mounted his horse and continued to follow the trail, hoping to track the culprit to his lair. His hopes were dashed when, once again, the trail merged into the main road, where it became indecipherable from others.

Conflicting emotions warred within him. One side of his mind relished the fact that he had to break off his pursuit. That meant he could return to town, where he now had some fresh information to talk over with Martha. The other side of his mind felt the bitter disappointment of one more failure to follow and identify the killer.

In the end, he lifted his horse's reins and headed back toward town at a swift trot. The sun was warm on his back. The wind was no more than the faintest of breezes. With every step of his horse toward town and Martha, the glow in his breast grew, and drew him more compellingly.

It may well have been the first time in his life he was so careless of alert attention to his surroundings. He saw the flash of the sun from something metal in a finger of timber that reached out toward the road. His eyes absorbed the information, telegraphing a warning to his mind instantly. His mind wasn't listening. It was elsewhere, dwelling on the auburn hair of Irish ancestry, studying the bridge of freckles across a perfectly shaped nose, eyeing the curves of the most alluring body he had ever beheld, tasting again the sweetness of rosy lips against his.

The message of mortal peril his eyes perceived hammered against the preoccupation of his mind with relentless persistence. The unaccustomed warm glow of his mind refused to consider it.

The human mind is a wonderful thing. It processes things with amazing speed. The eyes' message of warning and the mind's rejection of the message occurred, recurred, repeated, echoed again in the space of less than a heartbeat.

At long last, against his will, the message made its way through the reluctance of his joyous reverie. He jumped with a terrified start as he realized that message's import, and his own reluctance to respond instantly to it. He leaned forward and to the side, grasping the stock of his rifle as it rode in its saddle scabbard.

At the same instant a wisp of smoke appeared at the edge of the trees. He felt a tug at his shirt, just below his left arm.

He never hesitated. He whipped the rifle upward and snapped off a shot at the spot in the trees where he had seen the puff of gunsmoke. Even as he did, he rammed his spurs into his mount's sides, sending the horse lunging forward, directly toward the source of the threat. The angry whine of a second bullet passed perilously close to his right ear.

As he approached the timber from which it had come, he heard the crashing of brush and branches as his stalker fled. Heedless of danger, he bent low over the saddle horn and nudged his horse through the trees and brush at a reckless pace.

In spite of the faithful mount's willingness and effort, ducking and dodging through the timber slowed him considerably. When they broke into the clear at the other side of the timber, he caught just one fleeting glimpse of his quarry as he disappeared over a ridge. Something about him, the way he sat his horse, his silhouette against the sky, something, rang a faint bell in his mind. It was just one glimpse, just a fraction of a second, not nearly enough for him to be able to identify, even though there was something tantalizingly familiar about him.

Staying as low in the saddle as he could, he aimed for the spot as swiftly as the horse could navigate the broken terrain. He well knew the killer might turn at any point and wait for him to appear, shooting him before he could react. He gambled that his tactic of instant attack had rattled him enough to ensure that he would continue to flee instead. At least he fervently hoped so. If he was wrong, he would die, as so many had before him, at the hands of this ruthless rifleman.

As he crested the ridge, his eyes darted about, seeking any sign of the gunman. Nothing moved.

Warily, he hastily dismounted and studied the land before him over the top of his horse's neck, keeping as much of himself sheltered by the animal as he could. Nothing moved.

He visually traced out at least four possible routes beyond the spot where he stood, which the man might have taken. He had no way of knowing which had the greatest possibility.

The ground was hard and rocky, betraying almost no tracks. He could follow a trail like that, but it was slow, painstaking work. By the time he'd determined which way the sniper had gone, he would once again have blended his tracks into all the others on the main road, or carefully followed bare rock far enough to ensure he would not be followed.

He swore softly under his breath. Climbing back into the saddle, he retraced his path to the spot from which the shots had come. Dismounting, he paced slowly and carefully in a grid pattern, until he found what he sought. Bending over, he picked up the empty brass from one of the bullets that had been intended for him.

'Well, at least I know the caliber of his rifle,' he muttered. 'Thirty-thirty. I thought he was probably using a .44-.40, or maybe a .50, accurate as he is at long range. Thirty-thirty. Well, at least I know that much.'

It was a small consolation.

On the brighter side, there was now nothing to prevent his return to Deadwood, where Martha waited. Her reaction when he showed her the hole in his shirt more than compensated for the threat he had survived.

CHAPTER 17

'Brigands! Bandits! Killers! Ver ist der Sheriff? I need helps! *Schnell!*'

If it were not for his obvious terror, it would have been a hilarious picture. He sat on his galloping horse, feet free of the stirrups, splayed widely for whatever balance they could provide. He bounced high enough from the saddle with every stride of the horse to see daylight beneath him. With one hand he held on to a fedora he had smashed down on to his ears. With the other hand he held the reins at shoulder height. An ornate vest billowed out on either side of him, giving the impression of auxiliary wings that vainly sought to lift him airborne.

They would have had to have been stout wings indeed to have done so. He weighed nearly 300 pounds. The muttonchops sidewhiskers and moustache added to his comical appearance.

Alerted by the strident cries for help, Marshal MacLauren stepped into the street. Cole and Martha, inseparable it seemed these days, were right behind him.

As the man skidded his horse to a sliding stop in a cloud of dust, MacLauren grabbed the animal's bridle. The rider tumbled from the saddle, sprawling in the dusty street.

He hastened to his feet, oblivious of the dirt with which his fall had covered him. With an accent that nearly defied their attempts to understand, he puffed breathlessly, 'Ve haf beened attackted. Ve haf been shot at. Mine guards ist habben been shotted. Mine horse ist been shotted. I haf been robbed!'

'Whoa, whoa. Slow down,' MacLauren soothed, trying to lower the man's level of agitation. 'Who are you?'

'Mine name ist Baron von Rothchilder. I haf been robbed.'

'Who robbed you?'

'It vas robbers. Brigands. Killers. Dey haf shooted from behind some rocks, and shooted mine guards. Mine guards, dat vasn't shotted too quick, shotted back, but dey vas all shooted. Mine carriage vas not so fast enough, und besides, that horse vas shotted too, so I used vun of mine guard's horses, und got avay. I come here as fast as I can come, so someone can help.'

The story, in spite of its unique delivery, was old enough by now to be both trite and infuriating to all three of his listeners. By the time he finished his story, a small crowd had gathered.

MacLauren took a deep breath. He addressed the crowd. 'Somebody take this fella over to one of the saloons and get him a drink. We'll ride out and see what we can find.'

'Ach! Dat ist so good a sound. A beer vould taste so goot, yoost now.'

'I'll go get my horse,' Cole volunteered.

MacLauren just nodded. Martha said, 'I'll get Father's and mine from home. I want to come with you.'

Alarm surged within Cole. The thought of Martha riding deliberately on the trail of this cold-blooded killer was more than he could deal with. 'That ain't a good idea,' he said.

Seth MacLauren's face abruptly transformed from one of grim determination to one of wry amusement. 'Good luck talkin' her out of anythin',' he muttered, as he walked back into his office for his rifle.

His words were not only accurate, they were prophetic. For just an instant, Cole had the vision of a life with a woman whose will was every bit as strong as his own. Strangely enough, it seemed in that moment more of an attractive challenge than a deterrent.

As he left the livery barn with his horse, Gideon met him.

'You heard?' Cole asked, without preamble.

'I's heard,' Gideon responded. 'Y'all is gonna try trackin' that fella agin?'

Cole nodded. 'Doesn't seem like we've got a whole lot of choice.'

'Ain't got a whole lot o' promise neither,' Gideon opined.

Cole shrugged. 'It hasn't paid off yet, anyway.'

'Them fellas out there's all deader'n doornails,' Gideon offered.

'No doubt.'

'Trail's jest gonna peter out in the rocks again.'

'More than likely.'

'What you needs is a good hound.'

'A what?'

'You needs a good hound dog what kin track 'im.'

Cole studied his friend. 'I've never been around hounds, but I've heard of 'em. Doesn't a hound need something that belongs to a person to get his scent?'

'A good hound don't. He kin pick up a scent pertneart anywheres, an' foller it.'

'Are you saying a hound could track this guy?'

' 'Course he could,' Gideon assured him. 'A good hound kin track a fly across bare rock after four inches o' rain an' a cyclone come through.'

Cole chuckled. 'You ain't stretchin' things just a bit, by any chance, are you?'

'Only a teensy little bit, maybe. They really kin track, though. Hunters has been usin'em to track any o' my folks what escaped fer as long as they's been slaves in this here country. Once the hounds get your track, there ain't nothin' 'ceptin' ten miles o' swamp water what'll throw 'em off the scent.'

The irony of the situation ran through Cole's mind briefly. Here was an ex-slave, recommending exactly what he must have lived in fear of most of his life. The thought sent a shudder through him, but he dismissed it determinedly. 'It'd be worth a try, I suppose, if we just happened to have a hound.'

Gideon's grin threatened to engulf both ears. 'That there's 'zactly what I ketched up with you to tell you. I's got a friend down the gully a ways. Well, it's Lily Mae's pa. That's who it is. Lije Tillman. Tillman's Lily Mae's last name. Anyway, Lije, her pa, he's got this here Blue Tick Coon Hound what he says got the best nose he ever seen on a dog. I's bettin' he'll be plumb tickled to loan him to me.'

'He's OK with you bein' sweet on his daughter, is he?'

Gideon continued to grin from ear to ear. 'Oh, he's plumb more'n OK with that! Thanks to you, I's the first darky he's ever seed what's got some money an' a chanst to 'mount to somethin'. I 'spect as how he figgers if'n Lily Mae an' me get hitched up, he'll end up gettin' took purty good care of too.'

'You wouldn't be buyin' a bride, now, would you?' Cole teased.

Gideon's chest visibly puffed outward. 'I doesn't need to buy Lily Mae,' he declared. 'She was plumb head over heels in love with me when she still thought I was a penniless darky swampin' in Number Six.'

'Must be what comes from being so handsome and dashing.'

Sensing no irony or sarcasm in the statement, Gideon simply beamed. 'It's a problem I's willin' to deal with.'

Cole brought the conversation abruptly back to the present. 'So how long will it take you to get the hound?'

'It'll take me maybe fifteen minutes is all.'

Cole nodded. 'OK. We'd just as well give it a try. Nothing else has turned up anything.'

Gideon hurried away as Cole turned back to inform Martha and her father of the change in plans. More than ever he did not want Martha along, but he had the sinking feeling she would be riding with them, whether he was comfortable with the idea or not.

An hour later they warily approached the scene of carnage. Five men lay sprawled on the ground. Four of them had a weapon close to a dead hand. The other had not even had opportunity to draw a weapon. Four had each died from a single shot. The fifth was wounded in the leg, and had a small round hole in the center of his forehead. Powder burns indicated the killer's gun was placed almost against the skin before the trigger was pulled.

'Look at that!' MacLauren fumed. 'He must've been the last man alive, and him wounded. He threw down his gun and surrendered. The killer walked right up to him, stuck his gun to his head, and blew his brains out. When we catch this cold-blooded ba— Sorry, Martha. When we catch this guy, I'm gonna hang him by inches, pullin' the rope up a little at a time, just to give him plenty of time to think about every person he's sent to kingdom come without a chance.'

Martha was aghast. 'Father!'

'Well, wouldn't you?' the marshal demanded, chin jutted forward toward his daughter.

She opened her mouth to respond, then closed it again. She would never have admitted the kinship her father's words found in her own soul.

Two horses lay dead on the ground, in addition to the one still harnessed to the chaise in which the count had ridden.

'He missed a lot of stuff, this time,' Cole announced.

Together they looked at the remaining contents of the German count's chaise. A heavy strongbox remained on the floor, its lock intact. Several other items, including several articles of jewelry were strewn about the seat and floor. Martha picked up a heavy necklace. 'This is really heavy. It must be almost pure gold.'

'I'll bet that's a real ruby in it too,' MacLauren added.

'Count on it,' Cole agreed.

Gideon interrupted the conversation. 'Where's you want this here hound to commence?'

Cole looked around thoughtfully. 'I'm guessing he was holed up in that bunch of rocks over there. If we start from there, will he pick up the right scent and follow it?'

'Count on it,' Gideon echoed Cole's earlier words, even down to the exact tone and emphasis.

He proved as good as his word. The other three trailed along as Gideon led the dog to the rocks. Straining at the leash Gideon held, the animal eagerly snuffled around on the ground. 'Track, Nimrod,' he commanded.

The hound began to work in ever-widening circles, his nose to the ground. Gideon was hard-pressed to keep up with him, as he strained against the leash. After no more than two minutes, the hound lined out directly toward the scene of carnage, nearly a hundred yards away.

'He's done got the scent!' Gideon's triumphant shout confirmed.

Cole grabbed the trailing reins of Gideon's horse. He and the two MacLaurens followed, as Gideon ran to keep up with the excited hound.

When they approached the bodies strewn on the ground, Gideon hauled back on the leash, keeping the dog away. Instead of allowing him to ramble through what would certainly be an overlapping and confusing trail, he led the reluctant animal in a circle, well outside of all the confusing scents of death and blood and fear.

A little more than halfway around the circle, the hound again alerted to the scent. With loud baying, he began to pull against the leash, straining to follow some wisp of scent only he could detect in the sharp air.

'He's got the scent,' Gideon called. 'Want me to turn 'im loose?'

'Don't we need to tend to these dead men first?' Martha objected.

'They ain't goin' nowhere,' Seth declared with unaccustomed callousness. 'We'll pick 'em up and take 'em back to town after we find out where this trail leads.'

'Let him go then,' Cole told Gideon.

Gideon removed the leash from the dog and bolted to his horse, leaping into the saddle. By the time he hit the saddle, the hound had begun baying, nose to the ground, following the invisible tendril at an eager run.

The four followed, keeping their horses to a rapid trot, sometimes having to lift them to a canter to keep up with the eager and exuberant dog.

The trail led across a gravelly ridge, then down into the bottom of a shallow draw. As they rode past, Cole caught a glimpse of two separate fresh tracks. He nodded with satisfaction, confident the dog was, in fact, following the trail of someone on horseback.

A quarter of a mile down the draw the trail led up the side, following a deer trail. At the top it began to angle almost directly west. The direction it was going would skirt Deadwood to the south.

The dog neither flagged nor slowed. His baying kept up a constant refrain of certainty and excitement.

They followed along beside a small creek for nearly a mile, its merry babble providing a counter melody to the music of the hound.

From time to time Cole caught further glimpses of the tracks left by the horse the dog followed. Once, a clearly defined track showed the now-familiar imprint of the broken horseshoe. There was no mirth in his tight smile as he confirmed they were on the trail of the killer.

Well past Deadwood, the trail veered back slightly

to the north. The hills began to flatten out perceptibly. The timber thinned. They were once again able to see some distance ahead.

The dog never faltered from his tenacious pursuit of his unseen quarry.

Suddenly Martha's horse stumbled and pitched forward. At almost the same instant Cole spotted a small puff of smoke from a brushy outcropping some distance ahead. Martha screamed as she flew forward over the head of her horse.

She tucked her shoulder and rolled when she struck the ground, as if she had been flung from a dozen horses before. With no hesitation, Cole spurred his horse to her. 'Grab my hand!' he yelled.

As if they had practiced it a dozen times, she grabbed his sleeve as his iron grip closed on her wrist. She leaped, pulling herself upward as hard as she could. The combined lift of both their arms, combined with the speed of his horse, had the effect of vaulting her upward, on to his horse just behind the cantle of his saddle. Her arms instantly locked around his waist.

'Head for those rocks!' Cole ordered.

He needn't have bothered. Both Seth and Gideon had already spotted the possible cover, and were heading their horses that way on a dead run.

Dirt and gravel kicked up twice just beyond them as they scrambled to the shelter of the rocks. Seth and Gideon dived from their horses, rifles in hand, and began to return fire, firing blindly into the brush from which the attacking shots had come.

131

Approaching the rocks, Cole shouted, 'Jump down!'

Martha complied at once, flattening herself on the ground behind the nearest boulder.

Cole spurred his horse, rather than dismounting. Hugging the saddle horn, he ran his mount at an oblique angle, seeking to flank their quarry, who had become their hunter.

It was a bold move, calculated to draw fire away from the others, especially Martha. It was not a smart move. The object of their quest was an excellent marksman, well positioned, with a field of fire that allowed him to take careful aim to thwart the attempt to flank his position. Cole was, in that moment, just as good as dead. He realized his error in judgment with a sinking feeling, as he hugged his horse's neck and braced for the hot leaden projectile that would end his life.

Five people forgot a faithful dog. The dog did not forget he had been sent after quarry, as he had been well trained to do. The hidden gunman fired the fourth shot at his pursuers just as seventy-five pounds of Blue Tick Hound barreled into him, knocking him sprawling on the ground. The shot intended for Cole soared off harmlessly into empty air.

The gunman cursed viciously, slamming the butt of his rifle stock into the head of Nimrod the hound. The dog yelped once, and stretched out on the ground, where it remained inert.

The gunman turned his attention back to his pursuers at once. The dog's intervention, however, had given Cole exactly the opportunity he needed. Seeing a potential spot of cover, he dived head first into a shallow depression behind a large clump of soap weeds.

He would have been hard-pressed to find more effective cover. Although he could not move away from the spot he nestled down into, he was well shielded from the killer's rifle fire. More important, he could peer between blades of the soap weed and see, with little chance of being seen in return.

His horse had run on several yards and stopped, and was now tearing off bites of dry grass. The peril of his rider was no longer his concern.

Seth and Gideon kept up a steady, probing fire into the brush from which their attack had come. Cole watched the spot over his rifle barrel, waiting patiently for the opportunity he knew must come.

The stand-off continued for nearly an hour. An occasional shot from each side continued to confirm for each the presence of the others.

Perhaps, Cole thought, if he maintained silence long enough, the killer might forget about him. Maybe the man would even decide Cole had been hit, rather than diving voluntarily from his saddle. Perhaps he would just get careless.

Once he thought he caught a glimpse of movement. His finger twitched instantly. His rifle fired. Then the glimpse was gone. The man disappeared.

Did I hit him? Cole asked silently.

There was no answer. Time dragged intolerably.

He waited for twenty minutes. It seemed like hours. The occasional probing shots from his friends evoked no response from the brush.

He raised his head as much as he thought he dared, and looked around. A dozen yards to his right, and closer to the brush, a large rock offered a spot of cover. Moving swiftly, he came to his feet, crouched low, and ran for it. He dived behind it, waiting for the whine of a bullet, hoping he would be alive to hear it buzz past him. There was nothing.

He peered from around the side of the rock. Nothing moved. Spotting a small clump of brush, inadequate at best for cover, but alone in offering anything, he again sprinted forward and dived out of sight. Nothing happened.

He eyed a half-dozen trees close together more than twenty yards away. Once in those trees, he would be effectively behind their assailant. The only problem was twenty yards of open space between himself and their protection.

Without thinking about it any longer, he sprinted from his cover, running a zigzag pattern, until he reached the trees. There was no pursuing rifle fire.

Well, either I got him, or he's lit out, or he's low on ammunition and waiting for a clear shot.

He began to move forward cautiously, hoping one of his friends wouldn't catch a glimpse of his movement and shoot him by mistake.

With utmost caution he moved like a silent shadow through the thick timber and brush, careful to move each small branch of brush around himself so it would not emit a betraying swish or crack. Peering around the trunk of a large tree, he could clearly see an area of well-trampled grass and brush. The killer's tracks were obvious. There was no sign of the man himself.

Still moving with extreme caution, he followed the faint trail of the man's exit from his position. Less than a dozen yards away the tracks announced that he had mounted his horse and ridden silently away while they felt themselves pinned down. The woods were empty.

He stepped to the edge of the timber, shouting his identity before he exposed himself. Then he stepped into the clear and motioned his friends to join him. Even as he did, the now familiar feeling of failure twisted a tight knot in his gut. They had been so close. The idea of a hound tracking him had worked so well. He had escaped anyway.

CHAPTER 18

'I is so glad he ain't plumb dead! I don't know what I'd tell Lije if'n I went an' got his dog kilt.'

Gideon sat on the ground, holding the hapless hound. When Cole had shouted to the others that their assailant was gone, Gideon had come on a run. Tears streaming down his face, he cradled the dog's head. He whipped off his neckerchief and began to mop the blood from the dog's skull, moaning over the large lump.

Almost as if waiting for that attention, the dog began to respond. His right front toes began to twitch. A soft whine escaped from his slack mouth. As Gideon continued to cajole him to react, his eyes fluttered open. His tail began a slow sway back and forth.

'He's alive!' Gideon exulted. 'He's still alive!'

In another context it would have seemed ludicrous indeed. Martha flew into Cole's arms, and they held each other for a long moment, murmuring words of reassurance and joy that each was still alive and unhurt. Then four people breathlessly gave a scrawny hound their full attention. Gideon's glee was reflected in the faces of all three of his friends.

'Looks like he must've gotten clubbed on the head, instead of shot,' Seth opined.

'Thank goodness for that, at least,' Martha echoed.

'Probably used his rifle butt when the dog came at him,' Cole guessed.

'He'da shore took 'im down, ol' Nimrod would,' Gideon assured them. 'He was on his scent, and he wouldn'ta stopped till he barreled into 'im. He'da like to tore 'im apart, if'n he hadn't got hit on the head thataway.'

Cole strode back to the tracks of the horse that had patiently awaited his master. Studying the ground carefully, he gave a grunt of satisfaction. 'Sure enough,' he announced. 'There's the busted shoe.'

Seth nodded sagely. 'Can't imagine anyone in this country bein' too cheap to have the blacksmith replace a busted shoe.'

Cole pursed his lips thoughtfully. 'Do you s'pose maybe he asked the smith and the smith wouldn't replace that shoe without doing all four. The shoes are all really worn.'

Martha countered the direction of his thoughts. 'But, but, if he's the one that's been killing and robbing so many people, why in the world would it be any problem paying for that? Just think of the amount of money he's stolen.'

Cole didn't respond. He was walking around the edges of the place where the gunman had set up the ambush of his pursuers. After some moments, on a patch of clear ground, moist in the persistent shade of the timber, he found clearly imprinted tracks in the ground. As he studied them, the hair rose along the back of his neck. The picture of a fleeing silhouette from days before clicked into place in his memory. Understanding flooded through him. He softly called Seth MacLauren to his side.

He pointed to the tracks. Seth looked at them, then, frowning, at Cole. 'Does that mean what I think it means?'

'It has to,' Cole affirmed. 'Do you know more than one man in this country who wears boots with holes that size in the soles?'

Seth shook his head. 'Only one.'

'That would make the broken horseshoe make sense too,' Cole continued. 'He's the only man I know too cheap to take good care of his horse.'

'So what are you gonna do?' the lawman asked.

Cole had already thought it through. 'You three take the dog and go back to where the baron's guards are. You and Martha can ride double that far. Load 'em into the chaise and haul them and the dog into town. Then ride out to his place. I'll meet you there.'

'What are you gonna do?' Seth repeated himself, even though he already knew the answer.

'I'm going to hightail it straight for his place. He'll most likely ride an indirect route, and try to hide his trail, because he knows we'll try to track him from here, but won't know we've figured out who he is. If I ride hard, I can probably get there ahead of him. It's high time he got surprised for a change.'

Without waiting for an answer, he sprinted to his horse, mounted, and rode away at a swift canter.

Seeing him go, Martha's face flushed, then paled, then flushed. She hurried to Seth. 'Father! Where is Cole going? He didn't say a word to me. He didn't offer me any explanation, or say goodbye or anything.'

The marshal studied the face of his daughter, which was growing more offended and angry by the second. 'He asked me to tell you,' he lied. 'He didn't want to take the time. He's figured out who the killer is. He's gonna try to get to his place ahead of him, then set up to surprise him.'

Martha's anger faded to fear instantly. 'By himself? Alone? I'm going after him.'

Seth grabbed her arm firmly. 'You can't do that. You'd only give him one more thing to worry about. He'd be more concerned about protecting you than keeping himself alive. Besides, you don't have a horse. Remember?'

'So what are we going to do?' she demanded. 'Just stand around here?'

He studied his daughter a long moment, his emotions alternately prompting him to chuckle or shake his head in frustration. At last Seth said, 'Well, let's get the dog back to town. We'll clean up that mess the killer left on the road back yonder. Then we'll put together a bunch of men and ride out to help Cole, just in case that man of yours needs any help.'

Gideon was not part of the conversation. His full attention was devoted to Nimrod. Martha retrieved the pair of their horses that had survived the killer's bullets. Only then did Gideon appear to even be aware of their presence.

'I's gonna get on my horse,' he announced. 'Then maybe you can hand Nimrod up to me.'

Martha looked at the dog and nearly burst out laughing. Gideon had carefully tied his bright-red neckerchief around the dog's head, in an effort to bind up the animal's wound. When he knotted it, it looked for all the world like a red bow, slightly askew, that a child would put on a pet while playing dress-up.

Seth turned away momentarily to conceal his own laughter. Gideon didn't even notice. Seth scooped up the still semi-conscious dog and handed him up to Gideon. He took him tenderly, carefully nestling him between himself and the pommel of his saddle. Totally ignoring all else, Gideon headed his horse at a slow and careful walk toward the waiting macabre chore with the baron's guards.

When he was safely out of hearing, Martha said, 'I'll bet he'll ride around every rocky place on the road so he won't jostle the dog too much.'

'He'll take care of him all right,' Seth agreed.

He tried not to resent Gideon's preoccupation with the dog as they returned to the scene of the

140

earlier carnage. He and Martha removed the harness from the dead horse that had pulled the Baron von Rothchilder's chaise. He got Gideon to leave the dog's side long enough to help him heave each of the dead guards into the chaise. Then, hoping against hope that he would be amenable to the arrangement, they stripped the saddle from the largest of the guards' surviving mounts. The large Morgan gelding was easily large enough for a light draft animal, but they had no way of knowing if he had ever been so used.

Their luck held. Before they had finished harnessing him, it was apparent he had been there before, and didn't mind being harnessed.

Rather than ride in the chaise with four dead men, Seth used his lariat to tie a makeshift halter over the horse's bridle. He tied the reins to the seat of the chaise, just beside where he had persuaded the reluctant Gideon to lay the still groggy hound. Using his rope, he led the harnessed Morgan. Martha rode the mount of one of the dead guards. Gideon rode as close to the chaise as he possibly could.

They made a macabre procession as they filed into Deadwood. A town used to violence and excitement responded by pouring into the streets. Questions flew like feathers from a fight between two turkeys. Seth stoically led the procession down the street to the undertaker's establishment.

By the time they arrived there, Baron von Rothchilder, puffing down the street in pursuit of his chaise, caught up with them. 'Haf you gottened the brigands?' he demanded.

'No, but we know who one of them is,' the marshal assured him. 'I think it's likely that one is all there is.'

'Haf you gotten mine things dat he stoled?'

'Nope. He's still got 'em. He didn't have time to do anything with 'em.'

'Is he the one that's been doin' it all?' someone called.

'Who is it?'

Seth shook his head. 'I'm not ready to say for sure. Black is hot after him. I want ten men to mount up and ride with me. We'll head out and back up Black's play. He's sure he knows who it is, and he's on his way to his place.'

In less than fifteen minutes he headed out of town, accompanied by the ten men he had asked for.

A crowd watched as the swiftly assembled posse rode off down the street.

'I say, we ought to join them.'

Martha jumped at the unexpected voice at her shoulder. She turned to face Miles Masters. 'What?'

'I said we should join them. I would very much like to be in on the climax of this most exciting adventure. I have a buggy being harnessed to a horse just now at the livery barn. Would you care to join me?'

Martha could have hugged him. 'Try to stop me,' she said, grinned.

Together they hurried to the livery barn.

CHAPTER 19

Silas Spivey closed the door of his root cellar and turned around. Fifty feet in front of him, Cole Black stood facing him. Spivey blinked several times. His brow furrowed. His eyes narrowed. He glanced nervously around, assuring himself nobody was there except Cole. 'I didn't hear you ride in,' he said.

'I left my horse around on the other side of the house.'

'The dog shoulda barked.'

'He's dead.'

'You kilt my dog?'

'Nope. He was dead when I rode up. He looks like he starved to death. Didn't you ever feed him?'

Spivey shrugged. 'Shouldn't have to feed a dog, if he's worth his salt. If 'n you have to feed 'im, he ain't keepin' the rodents an' such down around a place.'

'I don't see anything anywhere near your house that would hide any small animals. He probably ran out of any to hunt.'

'Well, then, he shoulda ranged out farther.'

'Most folks take better care o' their animals than that.'

Spivey shrugged again. 'I take care o' the ones what brings some money back in. A dog, he don't make a man no money. No sense wastin' money buyin' feed for 'im.'

Cole fought to come up with an answer he could give calmly. Before he could do so, Spivey said, 'What're you doin' on my place anyway? You're trespassin', you know.'

'It's over, Spivey.'

'What's over.'

'I know it's you. I'm arresting you for murder and robbery.'

Spivey's face paled. 'What are you talkin' about?'

'You'd just as well give it up. I've been tryin' for weeks to figure out who'd ride a horse with one busted shoe, and never have the horse reshod. I found a track at too many of the places you left your horse while you shot people in cold blood.'

'Lots o' fellas has a horse bust a shoe,' Spivey argued.

'Only one that would just stick an extra nail in it and keep riding the horse that way.'

'That don't make me a killer.'

'It sure tells me who the killer is, though. I already checked the corral. Your horse is still sweaty. You didn't even rub him down when you got back. And he's still got that busted shoe. What've you done with all the money?'

Spivey blinked several times again. His bony

shoulders lifted slightly. 'I didn't take nothin' anyone had any rightful claim to.'

'You killed all those people in cold blood.'

'Most of 'em wasn't fit to live nohow. Bunch o' drinkin', gamblin', whorin' scum. Biggest share of 'em, leastways.'

'One of the ones you killed was the best friend I ever had,' Cole stated. 'Now unbuckle your gunbelt and let it drop.'

Spivey's bony shoulders lifted another notch. 'They'll hang me.'

'If they don't, I will. Now drop your gunbelt.'

'It ain't right to put a fella in a spot where he'll get hung without even a trial.'

'They may give you a trial. Then they'll hang you.'

'I ain't a good man to get hung. I ain't got a whole lot o' meat on my bones. Bein' lightweight an' all, I could hang a good while afore I die.'

'It couldn't happen to a better—'

That was as far as his words got. In an effort to catch Cole by surprise, Spivey gripped his pistol and whipped it upward from its holster with surprising speed. It was almost level when Cole's .45 roared. The slug from Cole's weapon slammed into his chest, driving him backward. He sprawled on the ground.

He pushed himself up on one elbow, trying to lever himself back up. He glared at Cole, and tried to lift his sidearm to bear on his nemesis. Neither effort was successful. He fell back on the ground. His gun hand flopped out to one side, releasing the weapon. His eyes stared unseeing into the darkening sky.

145

For reasons he could not fathom, Cole stood there staring at the bottom of the homesteader's boots. Most of the soles were worn away. Inside each boot, a piece of old leather had been cut to fit as an insole, and it, too, was worn completely through.

He glanced over at the corral. The mount Spivey had ridden all day stood there snuffling the ground. Not so much as a single pitchfork of hay had been tossed to him.

'Rode that horse all day, then gave him nothin' but post hay,' Cole gritted.

He holstered his gun as he walked to the corral. He took the pitchfork and started to lift hay from a nearby haystack. He stopped and looked at the pitchfork. He shook his head. 'One busted tine,' he muttered. 'Wouldn't you know it. Whatd'ya bet it's one somebody threw away.'

It took three efforts to get enough hay tossed over the corral fence with the flawed tool, but he satisfied himself the horse would have enough to eat once at least.

He carried four buckets of water from the hand pump and poured them into the water trough at the edge of the corral as well.

He walked back to the dead man where he lay, still staring sightlessly. 'I'd have rather seen you hang for what you did to Danny,' he said. 'But at least it's over.'

Weariness flooded over him. He went round to the front of Spivey's house, sat down on the ground, and leaned against the wall. 'When the rest of 'em get here, we'll see if we can find what you did with all that money,' he promised himself as he allowed his exhaustion to overwhelm him.

CHAPTER 20

Cole woke with a start. He hadn't even realized he had fallen asleep. It was totally dark. The sound of several horses indicated people's approach.

He suddenly remembered he hadn't replaced the spent round in his pistol after he had shot Spivey. Alarmed at his lapse, he quickly rectified the situation, returning the gun to its holster.

As he did, he remembered guiltily that he hadn't even cared for his own horse. He would still be standing where he had left him when he crept up to the house to surprise Spivey. 'Must've been tireder than I thought,' he remonstrated with himself.

The sounds of approach stopped. He pictured in his mind the group of people, nearly a dozen by the sound of their approach, sitting their horses, wondering if they dared approach any closer in the dark.

He stepped behind a corner of Spivey's shack, where he had some cover in case it was the wrong people out there in the blackness. 'Who's out there?'

he called.

'That you, Cole?'

The sound of Marshal MacLauren's voice sent a flood of relief through him. 'Yeah, it's me, Seth.'

'You find Spivey?'

'He's here.'

'Got 'im hogtied?'

'No. He's dead.'

In minutes he was fronted by MacLauren and the ten men he had brought with him, all merely dim shadows in the darkness. 'What happened?'

'I called him out. Told him the jig was up and we had proof enough to hang him. Told him to drop his gunbelt. He said he wasn't gonna hang, and went for his gun. He wasn't near fast enough, but I guess he won't hang.'

The thin sliver of moon gave barely enough light for him to make out each other's outline, so Cole could only guess at the effect his words had on the assembled group.

Silence hung as thick as the darkness for several seconds. MacLauren broke it. 'Did you find the money?'

'Didn't have time to look before dark.' He didn't add that he had been too tired to do so, and that, for the first time in his life, he hadn't even taken care of his horse. He suddenly hoped nobody would notice.

'So now what?'

Cole rubbed the back of his neck and head thoughtfully. 'Well, there ain't much sense fumblin' around in the dark. We'd just as well roll out our bedrolls and catch a little sleep. Come sunup we can see what we find.'

Without responding directly to him, MacLauren addressed the men. 'Just as well stick your horses in the corral, boys. Find a spot to roll out your beds and catch a few winks.'

Cole spoke up, 'There's a stack of hay just west of the corral, and a pump behind the house. The bucket's right by the pump, so you can feed and water 'em.'

'Somebody's comin',' a bodiless voice announced.

The group fell instantly silent, every ear straining to hear. The sound of a single horse, walking slowly and carefully in the darkness, and the creaking of a buggy indicated the approach of more people.

'Who's there?' MacLauren called.

'Father?'

'That you, Martha? What in Sam Hill you doin' out here?'

'Miles offered to bring me along, and I couldn't stand it to wait in town. Is Cole all right?'

'I'm fine,' Cole answered for himself, already moving to intercept the buggy.

'Oh, Cole! I'm so glad to hear your voice! Are you OK?'

'I'm fine.'

'What about . . . where is. . . .'

'Spivey's dead.'

'Oh, Cole!'

The buggy was beside him then, with Miles hauling on the reins to bring it to a stop. Even before it did, Martha lunged from the seat into Cole's waiting arms. Cole suddenly decided it wasn't going to be so bad waiting for daylight after all.

CHAPTER 21

Morning dawned sharp and crisp. Each tuft of grass, each twig of brushes and trees, each exposed area of buildings and fences, were coated with hoarfrost.

'It's so beautiful. I love mornings like this,' Martha murmured from Cole's shoulder.

The two had sat against the side of the dead homesteader's shack through the night. It was a solution that simply happened as the result of their ruling out other options. Still lost in the fresh, new wonder of their love for each other, they didn't want to separate for the night. Neither did they want to face the scorn and disrepute that would follow their sharing a bedroll, even fully clothed as they were. Especially with her father present, that seemed totally out of the question.

In the end they had simply sat down side by side, with their backs against the building, to talk. As the night's chill began to seep into their bones they retrieved their bedrolls, but they simply wrapped in them together, to continue their conversation. There they spent the night, alternately dozing, putting the wonder of their love into words, or planning how they were going to share the rest of their lives.

He hadn't actually proposed to her, nor she to him. From the time they both realized the love they felt for each other was returned, it seemed more as if they read one another's thoughts. The closest thing to an actual proposal of marriage came during one of their quietly murmured conversations between dozes, somewhere in the middle of the night.

'Do you want to be married by a preacher, or the mayor or a judge or someone?'

'I want to be married by a preacher. It just seems like that's the right thing to do.'

'It does to me, too. Do you care which one?'

She giggled. 'Like we have a choice? There are seventeen saloons in Deadwood, but only one church.'

He chuckled in response. 'It ain't exactly the Holy Land, is it?'

'Do you think it'll get better?'

'Sure. The gold will peter out. It always does. Then all the riff-raff will move on. Most of the business will go belly up, and those folks will leave. But the solid people, the ranchers, the few that end up with a mine that produces long-term, folks with money that just like this country – they'll all hang around. There'll still be a town, but it won't be more'n about a tenth the size it is now.'

She giggled again. 'One tenth. That'll only leave one-point-seven saloons in town. I don't know how a town can get along on only one-point-seven saloons.'

'Especially that point-seven one,' he agreed. 'That leaves most of one wall missing, and it gets pretty cold in the winter.'

For reasons only young people in love can understand, it was all hilariously funny. They laughed until they nearly cried, then fell asleep again for a while.

As daylight crept across the frosty land he stood to stretch the ache out of cramped muscles. She followed suit. They watched the rest of the posse slowly come to life and crawl out of the warm cocoons of their bedrolls. Somebody lit a fire in Spivey's stove and started a pot of coffee. The aroma that wafted across the yard stirred the last of the group from slumber.

Of all the group that had responded to the marshal's call for a posse, only Miles Masters had left town without a bedroll. The rest of them, accustomed as they were to the vagaries and severity of the weather, never left town without what they needed to survive long-term if they didn't make it back to town for a while. To tie the bedroll behind the saddle, or to throw it into a buggy or wagon, was as natural to them as saddling their horse.

Masters, on the other hand, had never become inured to the rigors of frontier life. To carry his bed with him, except on a planned hunting expedition or such, never entered his mind. He, alone, therefore, faced a long, cold night with no blankets.

'There's no reason you can't sleep in Spivey's

bunk,' Cole assured him.

Masters had eyed the pile of burlap and rags that Spivey had classified as bedding askance. 'I say, the small creatures that surely inhabit that rag-pile would bleed me dry and carry me off in little pieces by morning.'

'I doubt it. You can look it over and pretty well tell, but I doubt it's buggy. Spivey was tighter than the bark on a tree, but he was clean. I'm guessin' it's all as clean and free of bugs as the hotel bed I been sleepin' in. Probably better.'

'How would he even be able to rid them of bugs if he had chosen to do so?'

'Toss 'em in an anthill. Them red-fire ants will crawl through stuff and find every bug and every bug's egg that's there, and haul 'em off into their hill.'

'But how would one then get the ants out? I would think they would be worse than the things they are ridding the bedding of.'

'They all go back in the ground when it gets dark. You just wait till it gets dark, then pick up your stuff, with no ants and no other bugs either.'

'I say!'

Masters remained doubtful, but the chill of the night and the loneliness of being the only one awake soon overcame his reticence. He examined the various articles that made up the bedding by the light of Spivey's kerosene lamp, and found no evidence of lice, fleas, bedbugs, or other unwelcome livestock. He found the unsightly mess to be surprisingly warm and comfortable, and slept far better than he had anticipated.

It was he who suggested, 'Perhaps there will be a side of bacon or something such in the fruit cellar we could use to prepare breakfast.'

The words sparked Cole's memory, bringing his mind back from Martha, upon whom it had dwelt the entire night. 'That's where we need to start looking, anyway.'

'What?'

'We need to find out what Spivey did with all that stuff he stole. When I got here last night, he was just shutting the door on the fruit cellar. He wasn't bringing anything out with him, so he must have taken something into it. That'd be the first place to look.'

The words electrified the entire group. One of them grabbed the lamp out of the shack, and they moved en masse to the cellar door. It was flung open, then they all stood in a circle, as if unwilling to be the first to enter.

Cole stepped forward and walked down the steps, with Martha close behind him.

They paused at the bottom of the steps, to let their eyes adjust. Light spilled into the cellar from the door that opened upward, at only enough slant to allow rain water to run off. In spite of that, it was dim enough for them to have to wait until their eyes adjusted to be able to see.

The interior of the cellar was warm, in comparison to the sharp chill of the early winter morning. The smell of salt pork mingled with the scent of earth and an odd mixture of other odors. A small bin of potatoes, held off the floor on slats that allowed air to circulate, was nearly full. Aside from that, and the bin of curing salt that probably contained whatever cured meat was laid by for winter, the cellar appeared empty.

To the side, a pile of burlap bags, flour sacks and rags seemed to be all that was there.

'There's nothing here,' Martha breathed, as if unwilling to accept what her eyes were telling her.

'I say, he seems to have maintained a separate bedroom out here,' Miles joked, pointing to the pile of sacks and rags.

Something clicked in Cole's mind. 'He wouldn't be storing them here,' he pondered aloud. 'There always enough moisture in the ground to rot 'em, and he didn't waste anything. Let's see what's under 'em.'

He stepped over to the pile of sacks and picked up several from the top of the pile. A gasp passed through the cellar. It fed upward as a murmur of wonder and explanation to the rest of the posse who crowded the steps. Short words of description made real what those closest were able to see.

Beneath the scant cover that had concealed them, gold shone softly in the light of the coal-oil lamp. Gems set into heavy gold sparkled brightly. 'The baron's jewelry,' Martha breathed.

A set of saddle-bags was opened to reveal nuggets of almost pure gold, making them almost too heavy for Cole to lift.

Cash, gold, jewelry, watches, wallets, and one woman's purse, were all piled together. Every item that had been stolen was there, carefully hoarded, hidden beneath a nondescript pile of rags and used sacks.

It was Martha who put their thoughts into words. 'Why? There's enough money here for him to have lived like a king for the rest of his life, anywhere he wanted to go. But he didn't use it. He didn't spend any of it. He didn't really want any of it. He just put it here and hoarded it.'

'Maybe he was waitin' till he had enough, then he'd light outa the country with it,' an awed voice from the group offered.

Cole shook his head. 'Not likely. I doubt if he could have stood it, to buy a new set of clothes, all at once.'

'Why not?'

After a thoughtful silence, Cole said, 'I'd guess maybe he compared being poor with being good, so as long as he lived poor, he was good in his own mind.'

'Even if he was killin' folks an' takin' their money?'

'Maybe. Maybe he saw anybody with a lot of money as being evil, because they weren't poor like him. So it was his duty to kill them and take their money.'

'Thou shalt cleanse the land of its wickedness,' Martha quoted some snippet, having no idea where she had heard it before.

Seth MacLauren nodded. 'Could be, I guess. He

couldn't use it, or spend it, because then he'd be evil too. But by takin' it from them as had it, he was cleansing the land of wickedness.'

'That means he was as crazy as a pet coon,' one of the posse opined.

'There's not much doubt about that,' Cole agreed. 'I don't suppose we'll ever know for sure why he was doing it.'

'So what do we do now?'

'Well, let's get it all hauled out of here. Let's load it in the buggy Miles brought out with him. We can take it back to town.'

The thought of the one who had hired him to retrieve his money struck him suddenly. That money was almost certainly amongst the cache of plunder at his feet. 'We'll return all of it we can to the folks it belongs to.'

'What about those that's dead? We can't give their money back.'

They all pondered the question for a long moment. Then Marshal MacLauren said: 'We'll cross that bridge when we have to. Most of it can be given back to the families of them that was killed. It shouldn't even be too hard to find out who that prospector was, and where the wife and kids he left in Iowa are. That gold can be taken to them.'

'Give it to the darky to take back,' someone suggested. 'At least we know he can be trusted.'

The incongruity of the words struck Cole and Martha at the same time. Their eyes darted to each other's, as the wonder of those strange words being spoken aloud registered. Unable, or unwilling, to put their thoughts into words, they simply began picking up items from the pile of plunder, passing them along the line of men that stretched up into the sunlight.